Th

An Unusual ————— *Lain*

MW01503027

That Thing Called Love

An Unusual Romance ... And the Mumbai Rain

Tuhin A. Sinha

Srishti
PUBLISHERS & DISTRIBUTORS

SRISHTI PUBLISHERS & DISTRIBUTORS
N-16 C. R. Park
New Delhi 110 019
srishtipublishers@yahoo.com

First published by Srishti Publishers & Distributors in 2007
Copyright © Tuhin A, Sinha, 2006
New edition 2007

ISBN 81-88575-89-5

Typeset in AGaramond 11pt. by Suresh Kumar Sharma at Srishti

Cover photo: Ilona Yakovenko

Cover design: www.ettamina.com

Printed and bound in India

Dedicated

to

*those unsuspecting moments in life, which sometimes gather
to make a story...*

Acknowledgements

I'm grateful to Satjit Wadva, Shraddha Sinha, Ronojoy Chakraborty, Gajra Kottary, Hasmukh Gandhi and Ilona Yakovenko for their invaluable inputs to the book.

Anil Wanvari, Akshay Anand, Ashok Pandey, Atulya Sahay, Barkha Prabhakar, Jatin Khosla, Paromita Dey, Rajev and Delnaaz Paul, Rakeshh and Sunaina Paul and Subhash Sehgal (in alphabetical order) are some other personal friends whom I wish to thank. They may not have directly contributed to the writing or production of the book,, but have always been there for me whenever I needed them.

Gratitude is also due to my college and school buddies- Anant, Abhishek, Manish, Rahul, Vinesh, Vivek(in alphabetical order) and many more for some really interesting times and experiences we had together, which still provide me fodder for some of my stories.

Above all, I'm grateful to my parents Sh. Amarendra Kumar and Smt. Samira Sinha for the unflinching support they have always provided me to chase my maverick aspirations and my brother, Tanmay, who experiences a strange joy being my worst critic.

A Word or Two ...

The post liberalization era has seen radical changes in almost every sphere of our existence as a nation. There is an underlying consumerist streak in most things we venture into. Personal relationships are not untouched by this influence. The evolution of relationships, thus, has greater complexities imbued in it today. Besides, telling right from wrong has become increasingly contentious, thanks to divergent individual perspectives...

It has thus fascinated me to see how differently each individual views the issue of love, relationship and the institution of marriage.... "that thing called Love" is a journey of these disparate perspectives.

This book is about choices and the inherent dilemmas...Every human action that borders on the issue of morality is invariably borne out of a strong emotional propellant. The propellant in this story is the want of its characters to achieve that extra bit which they feel is missing in their *love story*. It is this unquenched want that triggers them on to face an interesting course of trials and tribulations...

"that thing called LOVE" is my labor of love. On TV and in films, my responsibility as writer is limited, what with it invariably being a collaborative effort. However, here I'm filled with a scary sense of responsibility to know that the 62,000 odd words of this novel are all mine.

Happy Reading!

Contents

1

Monday – Life Stinks!

It was Monday. The 10 km stretch leading from his house in Borivali to office at Andheri normally took Mayank exactly 25 minutes to cover. Today however, something seemed amiss. As he drove past the suburbs on his Hero Honda Splendor, Mayank felt unusually restless. One after another umpteen disturbances surfaced; he had barely covered half the distance when it already seemed like he had been driving for eternity.

The muggy conditions only added to Mayank's anguish. He was consumed with self doubt of various kinds. At every traffic signal where Mayank halted, he cursed the "timing". Yes, it was indeed a case of wrong timing, he conjectured; how else could he explain so many problems erupting, all too suddenly and simultaneously.

Mayank was, in fact, returning to office after a week's break. He had got engaged to a beautiful girl called Rewa in Delhi last week. He knew that everyone at the matrimonial website he worked for would demand a blow-by-blow account of it all. And that was the last thing he wanted to do!

While for many, the thought of beginning a new life of marital bliss would fill them up with vibrancy, it wasn't meant to be so for

Mayank. For him, this had only triggered off a thought process digging up various problems that had so far remained dormant in his mind. This engagement was not something of his choice; he had been persuaded into it by his Indore-based parents.

Was he prepared for marriage in the first place? Was Rewa the right girl for him in terms of temperament and resultant compatibility? Besides, can an arranged marriage hold in these difficult times? A plethora of such questions rattled him as he drove, often leading to momentary lapses in concentration. One such lapse had him skip a red signal at Kandivli; though it didn't cause an accident, it surely caught the attention of a constable, who gleefully scribbled his number, even as Mayank sped away, pushing away the thought of the inevitable, in ways more than one.

The fear of police interception made him drive much faster thereafter. But barely had he traveled a kilometer, when a strange disturbance held him up for almost 15 minutes. The local MP, Govinda was leading a huge procession of slum dwellers to protest against the demolition of illegal encroachments by the Government. Ironical, indeed, since he didn't seem to realize he belonged to the ruling party, thought Mayank.

The halt gave Mayank some breathing space; he was however invaded intermittently by digressive thoughts about Rewa, his fiancée and Ramamurthy, his boss. That over, Mayank drove further, only to realize that all traffic signals that he found clear on normal days were for some reason, conspiratorially red today by the time he reached them. Bad timing!

Whenever Mayank halted at a traffic signal, he never let go of an opportunity to peep into the bike mirror. His looks were one thing he was always conscious of.

Moments later, Mayank felt an unusual discomfort. He realized that a strange fear somehow lurked in his mind. On trying hard to figure out what it was, he deciphered that it was perhaps the fear of dehydration. He wondered why the thought had cropped up in his mind today and surmised later that it must have had to do with his profuse sweating. The mercury had soared to an uncharacteristic high of 39 even before noon and humidity must have been terribly worse. The uneasy state of his mind made the situation that much more repugnant as he bathed in sweat.

On his next halt at a Jogeshwari crossing, Mayank recollected having read an article in the Mumbai Times recently about the Bandra-Worli sea-link; he wondered if anybody had ever explored the possibility of some sea-link between Borivali and Andheri. It would save so much time, besides easing out the traffic in the suburbs, he thought. For a moment thereafter, he felt as though he had actually cracked a gem of an idea to solve Mumbai's traffic problems. But his ecstasy was short lived; for his mind-escape had resulted in a traffic chaos with the signal having got cleared and him still out there.

Still on his bike, he hoped that this excruciating heat would give way soon to the much awaited Mumbai Monsoon. This would be his first experience of the showers in Mumbai. He had heard so much about the rain and seen so much of it in Hindi movies that he was dying to experience it first hand. Now into the last week of May, he hoped that these magical showers would descend in the next couple of weeks. He momentarily imagined Rewa and himself getting wet in the rains, dismissed the thought and then consciously reined it in again. He was perhaps trying to ascertain whether the two of them would really look romantic together in the rains— perhaps the way Shahrukh Khan and Kajol looked in DDLJ. Anybody witness to these myriad journeys of his mind would surely have certified Mayank insane. Such indeed was the state of confusion that buffeted him even as he crossed Fame Adlabs, from where his office was barely a stone's throw away.

When Mayank entered office, he found it significantly decongested. About a third of the staff seemed to be missing. He was greeted with usual bonhomie by the receptionist, Tina, who with a perpetual wide grin looked immune to all external vagaries. Whilst Mayank could make out that something was amiss, he knew that Tina's grinning self would not be able to tell him what it was. He rushed in towards Anil's cubicle, only to find him missing.

"Anil Sir is in the big boss' cabin," a peon informed.

Mayank found it safe to just wait in Anil's cubicle for a while and take an appraisal of things from him, before being seen by the big boss. As he waited in the air-conditioned interior, he realized he was sweating even more than he did outside. He bit his nails in nervousness and stared blankly at a huge glass logo of thematchmaker.com that adorned almost the entire wall of the office on one side.

———

Thematchmaker.com happened to be the country's leading match-making portal. More than a million registered visitors to the website and success in having been catalyst to at least five thousand marriages worldwide is what the website proudly claimed.

Located on the second floor of a commercial complex at Andheri, the office space was small though reasonably well planned. It had a single entrance that almost bordered the reception area. The receptionist, a girl called Tina, was a cute little "airhead", perhaps just out of her college who could be really dumb at times.

However what she lacked in her mind, she more than made up with her infectiously sweet demeanor and camaraderie. She was in the true sense a charmer.

One part of the office had the marketing and the finance sections with four neat cubicles. One of these was occupied by Mayank, another by Anil, a CA, and a dear friend of Mayank. The other part of the office had a clutter of about a dozen girls, half of whom were into web designing and maintenance whereas the other half comprised those who were into support functions that included administrative responsibilities of collecting subscriptions. A small cabin had been carved out in the area behind the reception. This cabin was meant for the editorial team, comprising two people. Only one person though was on the job at the moment, and that was Vishal.

The office had a mezzanine floor that had a lavish cabin of the CEO. Just outside the cabin was a common enclosure with a TV set. It had a long conference table that was used for multiple purposes. While at times, the CEO could call important meetings there, at other times, he allowed it to be used by his staff for having lunch and sometimes even for watching cricket matches. A narrow set of wooden stairs connected the ground floor with the mezzanine floor.

The sound of someone walking down these steps arrested Mayank's attention as he waited in Anil's cabin. He was glad to see who it was.

'Hey, brother, good to see you back. When did you come?" beamed Anil, as he hugged Mayank.

"Just a while back...but what's up with Murthy? You never used to have these early meetings with him. Is everything okay?" Mayank's tenor was one of anxious concern.

5

"Well, yes, you know how he is… Mr. Tension! But forget him now. Tell me, how was it with you?"

"Good." Mayank looked preoccupied and looked around. "Anil," he said, "Why does the office look so empty?"

Anil pondered over the answer. "Well, as you know, after Stanley Corp withdrew its financing, things have been difficult for us. Last week, we were forced to offer a golden handshake to about a third of our people."

Mayank looked pale as though the premonition of a similar fate stared at him. After all, he was the Ad-sales manager of the website and ad revenues were meant to serve as the backbone for the organization.

The situation had been different a few months back, though. In fact, advertising revenues had formed an almost insignificant portion of the total revenues then. The primary revenue was, of course, the paid membership that the website offered to all its wide-eyed prospective brides and grooms. Not to forget the funding from a Singapore media magnate. However, of late, stiff competition had led to potential clients shifting over to other websites. There was also a problem with the financier; hence the website now had to undergo a paradigm shift and was driven almost entirely by sponsorships.

As Anil and Mayank spoke, they were invaded from behind.

"Hey, man, you're back!! Wow! Looking more dashing than ever! Looks like the Rewa effect, uhh?' exulted Vishal as he hugged Mayank, the hug seeming almost violent compared to that of Anil. Vishal, like Tina, was always carefree, irrespective of the situation. Unlike Tina, though, he held an important position in the website.

After a formal exchange of restrained pleasantries with his other colleagues, wherein they congratulated him on his engagement and he accepted the same rather faintly, Mayank sat down to chat at some length with pals Vishal and Anil.

Within moments, it was evident that, contrary to their perception, Mayank was quite hassled by his engagement.

"I don't know whether I'm doing the right thing by getting into marriage,' he confessed, 'I don't know the girl. Besides from whatever little interaction I had with her, she did not quite seem my type'....

"But what do you mean by your type?" probed Anil.

"Look, first of all, she is dusky, whereas I've always imagined my wife to be fair."

This was rubbished instantly by Vishal. "You must be crazy, man. Let me tell you that the sex appeal of dusky girls can never be matched by the fairer ones. Why does a Rekha or Bipasha Basu have men gasping for breath?" he asked and almost in the same breath answered, "It's because of the mesmerizing impact of their dusky persona. Besides from my personal experience, too, I can tell you that they make better partners in bed."

"Now how can you say that?" rebuffed Anil.

"Because unlike the fairer ones, used to being pampered by silly Indian males like us who are in perpetual awe of the fair skin, trust me, it's the darker ones who will go out of their way to fulfill our fantasies," Vishal retorted almost instantly, his confidence revealing his 'vast' experience.

Mayank thought for a moment before Anil broke the silence, unconvinced. "No yaar, I'm sure your research would do a sexologist proud, but let me tell you everything doesn't center round sex," he protested.

"You bet; it does. You might have temperamental differences

with your spouse but if she is great in bed, you won't look outside. But it will be a different story altogether if it's the other way round."

Mayank looked skeptically, doubting Vishal's judgment on a subject Vishal was known to have good authority over. He mulled over how temperamental differences could so easily be reconciled in bed. Wasn't temperamental compatibility a prerequisite for everything conjugal between man and woman? Mayank wondered.

Mayank felt quite convinced that for all his knowledge about the opposite sex, Vishal, for once had got his facts wrong. In the absence of temperamental compatibility, great sex looked a remote possibility. What if, for instance, one partner believed in intelligent foreplay whereas the other constantly rushed up things? Or what if one partner made stimulating conversation that enhanced the pleasure of physical advances whereas the other was quite dumb to respond? These were questions that could only be answered from practical experience, he surmised. But ironically, a first hand experience would have meant actually getting married—a prospect that was increasingly becoming more and more laden with perils for him.

Intending to break the impasse, Anil asked, 'Okay, so that was one reason; what is the other reason that makes you so apprehensive of Rewa?'

Mayank was speechless for a moment as though the fear of being ridiculed again had already surfaced in his mind. On being prodded again, he blurted, "I don't exactly know, yaar. But somehow when we interacted, she wasn't quite on the same wavelength."

'Why, what happened?' asked Vishal, with the stern directness of a seasoned constable.

"Look, to be honest, I felt she was pretty dumb. She didn't

have a clue about the U.S. presidential elections. Besides just to test her intelligence, I asked her about her views on capital punishment. And she looked at me as though I spoke Greek."

As Mayank narrated his story, he realized that Vishal and Anil were staring at him in much the same manner, amazed at his finicky behavior. 'Is there a person more intelligent than you on this earth?' ridiculed Anil. Vishal, on the other hand, broke into uncontrollable spurts of derisive laughter. "Were you by any chance under the impression that you were interviewing her for the UPSC exams?'

The office peon walked in at this point.

"Ramamurthy Sir wants to see you in his cabin immediately," he informed Mayank.

Sensing trouble, Mayank at once headed towards Ramamurthy's cabin somewhat akin to the conscription that army men on leave are expected to respect in the event of the sudden outbreak of war. Mayank and Vishal were for once in unison in their prediction that more problems lay in store for Mayank inside Ramamurthy's cabin.

~

Ramamurthy, the founder and CEO of thematchmaker.com was a stodgy, dark, bespectacled character. Though he was in his early forties, his insipidity easily made him appear ten years older. Ramamurthy had started off as a journalist in Chennai for a regional newspaper. It was in 1990 that an assignment had brought him to Mumbai, then Mumbai. He spent a couple of months in the city and chose to stay back.

An interesting story explained how he got into the match-making business. In his early days in Mumbai, Ramamurthy was often inundated with persuasive requests from his relatives back in Tamil Nadu, to find out suitable Mumbai based grooms for their girls. The difficulty that Ramamurthy encountered in answering this call somehow made him very cynical of the entire process by which families went about the exercise. He quite hated the fussy attitude he saw all around and as if to score a point, married the first decent girl his parents asked him to. He repented later, though. Within a few years of marriage, he separated from his wife.

Thereafter the Good Samaritan in him made him dwell even deeper into the exercise of finding the right matches. He applied his mind and eventually decided to start a match- making website in partnership with a friend, Rupani, who knew the nuances of the website business. For Ramamurthy, starting the website was almost like entering a second marriage. He didn't have any life outside the office.

That Ramamurthy would have summoned Mayank to congratulate him on his engagement was extremely unlikely; this Mayank knew from experience. But that had by no means prepared him for the ultimatum that Ramamurthy doled out:

"Yes, 15 lacs is what you have to collect. That too in two weeks' time."

Mayank, at first thought it was 5 lacs and that Ramamurthy had made a faux pas.

"And if you don't, then we're all doomed. The website will have to be shut down."

To say that the ultimatum came as an unexpectedly bad blow would be a gross understatement. But it manifested Mayank's fears of "Bad Timing!"

That night, tension kept Mayank awake till almost the wee hours of the morning. A flood of thoughts and images swam in his mind. He looked skywards into the rotating ceiling fan and felt his own life just moving round and round, as mundanely as the fan.

At various points, he tried to recall the exact words that Rewa had spoken and tried even harder to put two and two together and form a more definite notion about the girl. At other points he thought of the gargantuan target set by his crotchety boss. He surmised that he would jolly well have to start hunting for a new job right away. What about the bride? Was he really prepared to spend a life with Rewa? He did not know.

At times, he felt a strange sort of indignation towards his parents. After all, why did they have to force him into this marriage? Twenty nine, he thought, might look like having grown old enough for marriage in a small town but in a place like Mumbai, that is just about the time when money begins to flow in and the best of bachelor fun is supposed to start. However, as an afterthought Mayank also empathized with his parents. Hadn't they given him complete freedom to do whatever he wanted to in his career? Didn't they have a right to exercise some amount of control at least as far as the timing of his marriage went?

Mayank's parents had, in fact, given Mayank the liberty to choose a girl of his choice, as long as he did that within the stipulated time. It was only when Mayank kept dithering in his choice that his parents had to step in and arrange his marriage with the daughter of a family friend who had at one point been a colleague of Mayank's father.

Mayank lay on his bed, motionless; his countenance bereft of any definite expression or motive. He realized that it was already half past two in the morning. He straggled lazily out of the bed and took out a trunk from underneath his bed. He took out a diary from it that had an envelope tucked in its middle. He opened the envelope to take out a few pictures. With a pensive expression and dreamy eyes, he stared at the pictures as he laid them across his bed.

The pictures were from a bygone phase; a phase when he was in love, perhaps the one and the only time in his life. The pictures transported him into nostalgia; took him back to good old days in Delhi's Hindu College and to the realms of utopia. Multiple images of those good old days thronged his mind. The breezy wintry mornings in the University Campus where he would wait outside the college gate for Shweta; Shweta arriving from a distance in a cycle rickshaw, protected adequately with a thick cardigan or maybe two above her traditional salwar kameez, her cheeks glowing pink in the misty cold weather; then walking across the sprawling campus, the maroon brick walled college building lending congruence to a picture perfect semblance of serene romance; the annual college fest Mecca, where Shweta invariably won accolades and prizes for her singing and Mayank imagined her singing the same songs to him in the Alps of Switzerland; the last Valentines' Day that they spent together, mostly roaming around the streets of Connaught Place before going all the way to Priya to watch the night show.

The pictures formed the most beautiful part of his life even now, as long as he tried not to remember what was not captured on camera. That bit however could not escape recollection; so powerfully was it etched on his mind.

Shweta had taken him to her place at Kashmere gate to meet her father. A man in late forties, well built, betel chewing, pathan suit clad and with a thick moustache twisted upwards at both ends was how Mayank's potential father-in-law looked like. His

12

way of talking was even more peculiar, laden predominantly with vernacular accent. His words were razor sharp and ruthless.

"Jai Mata Di… Myself Ji, Bhatia, Mohanlal Bhatia. We are in the biziness of manufacturing watter pumps and importing… sarry.. sarry exporting to Gulf… Look sirji, everything in life is *sauda*— deal, you know, including wat you people kall love… I heard ji, tusi love my daughter and want to marry her… look sirji, it is very simple… tusi show me a bank balance of 5 lakhs in the next one year and I will give my daughter's hand to you… if not, then there are enough good *rishtas* coming for Shweta anyways… Jai Mata Di."

These were the words that still resonated in Mayank's ears when he thought of the encounter he had with Bhatia. How he wished that sweet beings like Shweta were blessed with more amiable parents. That meeting had more or less made Mayank foresee the inevitability of their romance ending on an anti-climatic note. For, till he had completed his MBA, it wouldn't have made sense to elope and marry. Not with Mr. Bhatia's 'sauda' for sure.

An admission into a Lucknow based Management Institute thereafter kept Mayank away from Delhi for two years. And a few months later, he was told by a common friend that Shweta had been married off to a guy in the States.

When he recalled the seven years that had gone by after Shweta went out of his life, Mayank realized that most things that he had ventured into thereafter were either out of repentance or angst or both. He also realized that in the absence of either of these strong emotions, he never quite felt sufficiently motivated to do whatever he did. Venturing into Mumbai, for instance, was borne out of the angst that Delhi's laidback culture had perhaps become too confining for him. He wanted to explore a new market, a new world. He wanted to be a maverick like before. Today, however, when he found himself juxtaposed between the twin dilemmas of saving his job and marrying an unknown entity, craving for 'utopian fantasies' looked like treading the realm of surreal once again.

That it was indeed a case of twisted timing was evident from the fact that even at this hour, there was unusual humidity in the atmosphere and the breeze virtually non-existent. Mayank flung his shirt off to beat this burden.

The monsoon was still sometime away. Bad timing!

2

Saturday – A Close Shave!

It was Saturday. Five days had gone by since the draconian Monday but not much had changed. Not a penny of the targeted sponsorship had been achieved; Mayank's confusion over life partner issues still prevailed; heat conditions remained unabated.

To think of it, the whole issue of Mayank, being forced into engagement with someone he didn't deem to be the 'right girl' was actually ironic, especially as he had been used to surfing the matrimonial site almost daily in the past one year. It was not as if proposals had not come for him or that he hadn't proposed to other girls; he had done lots of all that. In fact, reasonable headway had also been made in certain cases. The problem arose when Mayank would unfailingly look for every single virtue in one girl; when he would start looking for his Shweta.

Mayank went about the task of dating girls with a lot of planning. For example, he evaluated them on five different parameters— looks, intellect, nature, outlook and education/job. Needless to say, he would look for the very best in all these aspects; his expectations often exceeded the rational, thus causing disappointment.

Mayank's first brush with a wannabe bride from indianmatchmaker.com was with a girl called Prerna, almost a year ago. The profile was brief and the girl looked pretty in the photograph. Besides, the mention of her being an airhostess did excite him. Physical beauty, after all, was an important prerequisite in his search. Without wasting time, he approached the girl. And luckily for him the girl responded favorably.

Prerna was quite a contrast to Mayank. She was chirpy, fun-loving, uncomplicated, spontaneous and above all a 'natural'. She did not plan things the way Mayank did. She would laugh freely. They got along quite well for a while; perhaps it was a case of opposites attracting each other. They even met on Valentines' Day, though both shied away from being the first to 'propose.' Both were perhaps strategically harping on the friendship plank, hoping that the other would tread the extra mile of making a formal proposal. This constant, pregnant expectation of "you do it first" eventually started getting on Mayank's nerves. Somewhere, in his heart, he had made up his mind that Prerna was not wife material; instead she was just 'time pass.' This categorization had to do with the intellectual incompatibility issue; he realized somewhere that an airhostess would charm him, no doubt, but perhaps won't have the intellect to engage him in the kind of absorbing interactions that he liked.

It is strange that Mayank, like many other males had come to categorize women in two broad categories: one, the 'time pass' variety, who were the girlfriend sort, the sort one could date and have fun with; and the other, the wife material, in whom they saw the virtues of being mother to their children. Prerna, obviously, by his perception, belonged to the former. However, girls being girls, Prerna was taken in by the good-natured flirting of Mayank and instinctively got closer to him. But, Mayank, like most men might have, interpreted this friendliness as a gesture of the girl wanting something 'more'. Encouraged by Vishal, Mayank, made a pass at her... and that was the end of their 'friendship'.

"Bloody hell!" he cursed, "Why do these women suddenly start behaving like prudes?" Mayank had complained impulsively, only to be reminded that unlike him, other aspirants on the website were more serious about its rightful usage.

After that Mayank met a string of girls. With one, a fashion designer, whom he quite liked, things didn't work out because she was a 'manglik'. Mayank was quite cheesed on discovering this new horoscopic impediment. He even tried to align with his astrologer to see if things could be worked around to make the match possible; but in vain.

In yet another instance, the girl in question, a business analyst with a multinational, was candid enough to tell him about a past relationship of hers in the first meeting. While Mayank appreciated her honesty, he could make out for sure that the girl was yet to get over her past. And he surely didn't want to be another Anil; well, more on that later.

Finally another girl, a Research Scholar whom he liked, was rejected by his parents on the flimsy ground that she was about half a year elder to him. They couldn't accept a "bahu" who was older to their son.

These misses had left Mayank where he was— high and dry, at level zero of his search; till his parents, doubting his sincerity of purpose, had emotionally blackmailed him into getting engaged to Rewa.

⌒

Like Mayank, Vishal too was involved in a 'search', though of a different kind. Vishal was perpetually on the lookout for women who wouldn't mind a passing affair. A senior journalist with the website, Vishal quite relished dealing with women who were difficult; they imbued him with a feeling of being challenged. He would in particular be on the lookout for stories where glamorous women could be featured and later work his way into their personal lives. Thanks to his expertise on the issue, Vishal had, in fact, come to be known for some of his "legendary" quotes:

"Journalism is surely the best profession to be in, if you have to invade the close circles of celebrity females. They pamper you because they know how much positive publicity can do for them. And then, it's entirely up to men like me to see how I can manipulate the situation and screw around."

"There is only one way to deal with a female – charm (read seduce) her and you will have your way."

Vishal was a married man, though by his words and actions, no one presumed him to be so simply because of his tall, athletic physique, infectious, charming smile and ever ready flirtatious comments. In his early thirties and married for the last three years now, he was still 'extremely accommodating' towards women. The sight of a curvaceous female would evoke a strange, mischievous spark in his behavior, so typical of a college Romeo. He never let go of an opportunity for dalliance and was pretty open about it. He was a master in the art of brazen ogling and as Anil would often remark- *yeh bhaisaab to aakhon hi aakhon mein rape kar dete hai ladkiyon ki* (Our brother virtually rapes women with his eyes).

On his part, Vishal professed that the 'power' of the eye was infallible. He maintained that 'if you get the right eye contact that evokes the desired response from the girl, getting her to bed is no more than a practical detail.' He asserted his views with such confidence that all those who heard him wondered whether they were blind or their eye 'power' was not normal.

Indeed, there were some days when his confidence levels soared so high that he told people that there was no girl in this world who would not succumb to temptation; "One simply had to be at it constantly," he said. His opinion obviously gave the impression that he had scant regard for women, beyond seeing them as objects of carnal desire.

Few would have disagreed that Vishal could aptly be called a male chauvinist in the truest sense of the word. He often justified his weakness for women by confiding in close friends that it was due to his inability to get the 'right girl' in his wife. But if somebody even vaguely insinuated a probe as to whether he had been the 'right guy' for his wife, it would offend him. For all that he did, Vishal staunchly believed that his wife was not entitled to the same liberties as him.

Mayank quite despised this hypocrisy and made no attempt to hide it from Vishal. But for all these vices, few in the office would have disagreed that Vishal was 'otherwise' a great guy. He was ever helpful and his weird sense of humor would lead to ripples of laughter even in grim situations.

Vishal's views were in sharp contrast to Anil's. Anil, who headed the Accounts section, was by all means an average, nondescript looker. He was however, a sincere guy in all respects, whether it concerned his work or his commitments to friends.

Anil would staunchly maintain that most problems in a relationship had to do with unrealistic expectations. "The basic problem with most men is that they keep looking for the 'right girl'; whereas actually the girl you get is the right one for you," he maintained. Anil had been married for a little over a year. His was a love marriage with Rupali, a girl, whom he had nursed to bring her out of her heartbreak from her previous lover.

There was one day in the month-the first Saturday when all three, Vishal, Anil and Mayank would get together and have a blast – a ritual they had conformed to in the last five months or so. The trio would watch a movie together, often an X rated one, and follow it up with drinks and dinner. The bonhomie would normally extend to the wee hours of the morning. The dinner would be prepared by Vishal himself, whose finesse with chilly chicken won him plaudits, while Anil and Mayank would help him out like disciplined interns. The venue for this gig would invariably be Mayank's bachelor den— a one-bedroom-hall-and-kitchen in Boriwali's Rustomjee Enclave.

For Vishal and Anil, this would be an occasion to relive their good old days of bachelorhood. Vishal, in fact had got his wife to agree to this monthly 'concession'; his wife had given in realizing that on this particular day, come what may, her husband would prefer the company of his friends to her physical charms. Mayank, however, doubted if any wife would do so happily.

Anil was usually the unwilling accomplice on these night outs. Though he felt guilty for staying away from his wife one whole night, it was his wife who encouraged him on. Rupali would maintain that it was so important to give each other space in a relationship. "If spending a night out with friends chilled him out," she reasoned, "that would only work better for our relationship." Mayank often wondered if he would want a wife like Rupali or one who would exercise more control. For, from what he saw and gathered lately, his tribe didn't quite value freedom or trust. He was not sure if he would, after marriage.

Anil often wondered how Rupali showed such maturity and

had the attitude to 'let go'. Rupali's unflinching trust in him would make Anil feel a bit guilty whenever he took these night outs. Little did he know that this guilt would manifest itself all the more in the next few hours!

It so happened, that Vishal who was flustered because of a dressing down he had got from Ramamurthy ended up spoiling the dish he was cooking.

"Bloody hell, nothing seems to going right!' he complained, moving into the living room, where Mayank and Anil were surfing channels. Almost all news channels were beaming reports of the Maharashtra Cabinet having decided to close all Dance Bars in the city from the next week. They showed the Deputy CM, Mr. R.R. Patil making the announcement. Mr. Patil spoke with the angered passion of a crusader as though if he were launching a war against terrorism.

"Look at his expressions! I'm sure he has been ditched by some bar dancer." Mayank attempted to lace the situation with humor.

Vishal was in a foul mood. He mooted the idea of going out on a drive on the highway. He obviously had some plans in mind when he said so, which the others were not aware of. He drove straight to Vashi and led them into a Dance Bar, called Mehfil, startling both Mayank and Anil.

"Don't worry. The ban comes into effect from next week. Today, you can enjoy as much as you want," he reassured them.

Though Anil protested initially, the latent human thirst for indulgence eventually rendered his own protests mild and inadequate. He decided thereafter to flow with the situation. Mayank, on the other hand, was actually excited. He had heard so much about the Dance Bars of Mumbai. He had seen the movie Chandni Bar, when he was in Delhi and had wanted to see what these bars looked like. He hoped though he wouldn't come across stories as heart wrenching as the ones depicted in the movie. His only apprehensions, however, were the reports of police frequently raiding such places. Vishal allayed those fears.

"Oye, don't worry, yaar. The only reason I chose Vashi is because of its location. Being out of the way and away from town, it is free from all unnecessary hassles of the policemen. Besides, the girls are also damn obliging, no nakhras like they do in the city bars."

He led them inside with the confidence of a true leader. From the knowledge that Vishal had about these places, it was apparent that he had been to the place before. Mayank however decided against ascertaining it from Vishal himself, lest that should spoil the mood before an exciting experience.

When the trio walked in, they were greeted with formal handshakes by the waiters. It reminded Mayank of the protocol that diplomats of two nations follow before talking business. However, the difference over here was that the waiters wouldn't quite leave his hand after the handshake. Mayank soon gathered what they wanted when he saw Vishal dole out a hundred-rupee note to one of them. The waiter, in turn, promised to ensure that whichever girl Vishal chose would be sent to him, irrespective of whosoever else wanted her. As the waiter apparently entertained a similar expectation from Mayank, Mayank had to pull his hand out of the handshake with a sudden jerk.

Soon thereafter, the trio sat on one of the several sofas that bordered the dance floor. About a dozen girls enthralled them with seductive dance movements to sleazy numbers. One number that looked like a hot favorite here was *Babuji zara dheere chalna…* from a nondescript movie called Dum. These dancers didn't remotely match up to the killer charms of a Yana Gupta; they compensated for it, though, by constantly gesticulating that they were 'available'. Mayank realized that initiating contact with these girls was easy. All one had to do was express a definite intent to spend time with them. With this, the selected girl would come over. Once they came over, they could be either made to sit alongside in a cozy posture and warmed up for the night, that is if one intended to spend the night with them; or else, one could press their boobs, finger them, get titillated and let them go. He saw this happening on at least some three or four sofas. Not all of these girls looked happy though. One of them looked particularly agonized, even as the client smothered her with smooches and for every smooch handed her a ten-rupee note. When Mayank saw this particular sight, he felt ashamed for a moment. Did the act not amount to paid molestation if not rape?

In his preoccupation, Mayank hadn't realized that one of these girls, apparently, a Nepalese, was ogling at him. She stood a few steps away from him, her body half turned towards him; she stared backwards at him, with what would be called 'tirchhee nazar' in their parlance. The girl was far from beautiful and looked like a prostitute; she had a sensuous figure though and the way she was dressed, revealing more than concealing, she looked quite attractive actually. Her boobs were bulging out of her blouse, almost as much as Mallika Sherawat's did at Cannes. It was unlikely, however, that the girl would have had any transplant.

Mayank wondered if Vishal's knowledgeable takes on the eye contact emanated from his frequent visits to these dance bars. His rumination was cut short by Vishal himself.

"Come on, buddy. It's happening. Just match the girl inch for inch. Give her an equally shameless expression."

If what Vishal actually meant had to be done, Mayank would have to take his tongue out and rub it gently against his lips, looking lusciously towards the female. Mayank chose to simply ogle at her. After a couple of minutes of unproductive mutual ogling, the girl gathered that Mayank was a 'bachcha' or perhaps he wasn't quite prepared to shell out the bucks. She chose to concentrate on a more willing client instead.

On the other hand, Vishal, who had set his eyes on a tall auburn haired charmer, soon decided to give up the subtleties of eye contact for more carnal suggestiveness. He wooed in great style, this girl called Reshma, who spoke in English and claimed to have done her English Honors from Xaviers' Mumbai. The mention of Xaviers' did startle him for a moment, but he was so consumed with the mission to lay her that he chose to ignore it. Though the female claimed to charge 10,000 for an hour, she agreed to go with Vishal for a paltry 2500. Reshma warned him though that there would be no oral sex for that amount. Soon, Vishal was seen taking the girl away to one of the four small rooms cordoned off on the first floor that were meant for the customers to have sex with their chosen ones.

Left alone, without their guiding angel, Mayank and Anil felt orphaned for a moment. However, the cacophony of numerous customers hooting and making lewd remarks at their favorite girls never quite allowed their thoughts to meander and they decided to play on by calling a couple of these girls over, before all of the good ones were taken away.

Anil sat with a short and cute girl called Bijli. She spoke in a Bengali accent and Anil surmised that she was perhaps an illegal Bangladeshi migrant. That was enough to arouse his curiosity. And, since Anil had this knack for arrogating undue importance to himself, he actually interviewed the girl.

His questions went thus: *So, how old are you? How long have you been in this profession? Do you stay with your family? How much do you get paid?* The female hated such wastage of time and Anil realized it gradually. As against the other people, who doled out notes for every progressive sexual overture, Anil took out notes for answering his questions, one after the other. He was probing into her private life as though he would soon crack some sensational case. However, for every question she answered, her expression became progressively constipated.

Some distance away, Mayank had got a sexy ghagra-choli clad girl called, Shahnaaz to sit with him. Of course, he knew by watching Chandni Bar that bar girls seldom revealed their true name. Though Shahnaaz was eagerly awaiting his moves, Mayank was in a weird situation actually. On the one hand, the thought of Rewa was making him feel guilty. He just wanted to get out of the place. At the same time, the place was tempting enough in a strange way. From his first hand experience, he was convinced that there was no denying that these were actually sex bars. Okay, agreed, he may not want to go full throttle and screw a girl, but there were so many options available. For instance, he could press her boobs, feel and rub her bare back. Better still, if she allowed, he could finger her, though from above her clothes. But did he want to do these? He didn't think so, but then, the alcohol was already acting on him. Besides he knew from experience that through their journey back, Vishal would brag about his experience. Would Mayank be a mute listener then? Prodded by the girl, who charged a 100 bucks per act, Mayank actually did all that he could sitting there. The girl, fascinated by his cute looks, finally made her clear move by giving him a quick kiss on his lips. She had thought he would be elated but Mayank hated it. He almost puked.

Strangely, by the time his escapade was through, he was sitting aimlessly. Guilt had got the better of fun.

At about a quarter to three, the trio left the bar. Vishal was understandably bubbling with enthusiasm, Anil lost in philosophical thoughts, while Mayank was silently furious.

"Mind blowing, it was! Oh she just too good. I just wish they could train our wives to be half as innovative."

Vishal could sense Mayank's indifference.

"What happened, hero? Don't tell me you again drew a blank just like you do in tapping your sponsors?" he teased.

"Will you just shut up? There is a bloody limit to everything. I wish you would share this experience with your wife," Mayank blasted.

Mayank's outburst was quite unexpected. For a while a deafening silence prevailed. Anil could gather that it was not something that would have erupted out of the blue. Perhaps it had to do with Mayank's disapproval of the ways of Vishal, which must have been building up for sometime.

By the time Mayank reached home he was feeling ashamed of himself. The feel of the bar dancers' lips had set off some sort of allergic reaction. He almost hated his body as though it stank. It was not until he virtually scrubbed his body clean with warm water that he rested in peace.

He slept almost till noon the next day. He woke up at around eleven and since it was a Sunday, he chose to linger on in bed for some more time. As he surfed through TV channels, he seemed to feel that all news channels, more or less, dwelt upon places that seemed familiar. He concentrated harder and was overcome by shock when the news sunk in:

In a massive clean-up operation, the Mumbai police had raided nearly 50 dance bars and arrested more than a 1000 people the previous night. A lot many of these arrests were made at the Mehfil Bar, where raids took place at around 3am.

3

When it Rains, it Pours

Now into the second week of June, the twelfth day of June to be precise, the Rain Gods had shown up finally. It had been raining incessantly since last night with drizzle and showers interchangeably doing the honors. While there was general pleasantness in the atmosphere, it couldn't possibly erode the strong undercurrent of despondency. It was a Friday. Normally, Fridays would ignite the TGIF (Thank God! It's Friday) spirit among the employees but today it looked more like a Black Friday what with so many sunken countenances all around.

Today was the last day for Mayank to meet the sponsorship requirement. And with barely twenty percent of the target accumulated so far it looked highly improbable that the website would survive. Some in the office had successfully conditioned themselves to thinking what lay beyond. They had been promised that in case the website shut, they would be given a salary compensation for an additional couple of months. It was meant to be a sort of golden handshake. Secure in the knowledge of this sop, some of the employees were often seen surfing naukri.com rather than their own website. Today was an acid test for Mayank though. He was supposed to make a crucial presentation to an important client. The client was called 'Shagun.'

'Shagun', located at Worli, was probably India's first and only exclusive wedding mall that stocked everything concerned with marriages under one roof, from wedding accessories and gifts to trousseaus. Touted as a new lifestyle destination, the mall had been designed to give a hassle-free experience to the customers. And its success in the last couple of years had bolstered it to open up a chain of stores in other cities as well.

The gamut of Shagun's product line was indeed incredibly vast. It included Sherwanis, Kamarbandh (waist bands), Safa (turban), Jooti (shoes), Kantha (pearl necklace) among others for men and ghagra-cholis, embroidered sarees and sandals among others for women. All of these were marketed under the common brand name of Shagun. The latest additions to Shagun's products were furnishings specially designed for setting up new homes. In addition, Shagun was rumored to be foraying into designer beachwear for honeymooning couples.

With a product line like this to boot, Shagun had always been seen as an important potential advertiser. Their customer base, after all, was supposed to be more or less similar to the target audience of the website. However, for some strange reason the brand had never been tapped. Mayank had been told that his predecessor, a guy called Akash, had tried his best but the brand manager of Shagun, a lady called Revathi was next to impossible. She was supposed to be a snooty, ill-informed lady who had her own fixed notions of marketing and was extremely dismissive of the efficacy of internet advertising. After nearly having to persuade her on the phone, she had finally given Mayank an appointment today.

The unexpected freshness brought about by the showers gave Mayank an intuition that something unexpected could possibly lie in store for him. But soon enough, he jettisoned the optimistic vibes as they really seemed far out and so alien.

With the crucial meeting barely two hours away, the atmosphere in the office was understandably tense. The showers had only added to the gloomy ambience with a couple of women complaining non stop of how the potholes would only flare up now and make commuting difficult. Mayank, however, personally loved these showers. How he wished the website was not in such a precarious situation so that he would have enjoyed his first feel of the Mumbai rains in unencumbered spirits.

A few yards away, Vishal was busy doing what he was good at – ogling. The girls this time around, however, were unable to protest. They were the wannabe brides who had listed themselves on the website with hope and expectation. He stared particularly hard at a sari-clad girl for almost a minute before declaring, "She's going to be a delight on bed, I tell you." Anil, who stood nearby reading his daily forecast in Mid Day wondered how Vishal could make such far reaching judgments with so much conviction; he didn't dare to ask him the same for fear of being subjected to a long-drawn answer replete with exaggerated claims.

Vishal looked around to realize that Mayank looked rather worried. He did his bit to cheer him up. "If this website has to shut, so be it. There will be many other places where we'll find decent jobs and great chicks," he reassured. "Come here, look at these. Who knows you might find a better girl than Rewa…"

Many a times, Mayank wondered how Vishal could retain and get away with such defiant blasphemy; but soon concluded that some questions had no answers and were better left ignored. Moreover Mayank felt a strange restlessness in the office. He chose to make a move for the meeting right away.

It was a half past twelve already and traveling to Worli, which on normal days took about an hour would surely take an extra half hour in that rain, he thought. As the drizzle persisted, he chose to borrow Vishal's Santro, instead of going on his bike. Vishal readily obliged.

Mayank drove across, trying hard to focus on the meeting. How would this snooty woman called Revathi look like? Wasn't her name ironically 'soft' given the person she was made out to be? Would she be beautiful or ugly or simply nondescript? How old must she be? Would she be kind enough to give him a patient hearing or whether she'd be another bitch? He ruminated, even as the slow speed at which he was forced to drive led to a series of digressive thoughts.

Mayank knew from experience that when the going was tough, nothing could be more irritating than having to deal with a banal woman, the sort who would be egocentric and unabashedly cocky. He remembered one such experience when a female brand manager had pinned him down with an ad nauseam query as to why she should advertise on the website when a daily newspaper provided her far greater reach and cost efficiency. Mayank's persistent efforts to convince her with every possible logical reason bore no result. The fact that she spoke atrociously faulty English and was insolently disdainful had only angered Mayank all the more.

Mayank had always believed that grace ought to be a quintessential feature in a woman's personality. Any woman devoid of it created a very odious sentiment in him. He wondered how it must be to be the husband of such a female and felt that if he had a wife like her, he would surely have had to seek love in an extra-marital source.

Mayank's meandering thoughts, at that point, had made him look a trifle preoccupied and lost. And as if her contempt was yet incomplete, the female had the temerity to wrap up the meeting with the most acerbic remark. "Look sir, your mind is not in the meeting. Hence you must come again with better preparation," she had remarked with gross insensitivity. No sooner had she left than Mayank had unleashed a diatribe of the choicest invectives— something he was not in the habit of doing except once in a while when confronted by such horrendous women and men.

Morbid pessimism crept into Mayank as he recalled that experience. From what Akash – the previous advertising manager of the website had to say about Revathi, he knew she was not going to be very different. As Mayank thought about it, the bang of a thundering sound almost blew him out of his senses for a moment; it was the sound of a cloud burst. The rains were now pouring heavily and most unsympathetically. Visibility was just as bad. Having reached Shivaji Park and with still twenty minutes or so in hand, Mayank decided to halt for a few minutes rather than take a risk.

The heavy rains however had him holed up at Shivaji Park for nearly half an hour. While he waited for the traffic to clear, he was witness to an amazing sight. A horde of teenagers drenched completely in showers, was battling each other out in an exciting football match. They appeared invigorated several times over by the rain. One of them, the shortest of them all, led the way and scored two shrewdly plotted goals in quick succession. The spirit displayed by these teenagers against odds made Mayank feel slightly more confident.

Mayank reached the office of Shagun about half an hour behind schedule. Shagun, the mall was located on the ground floor of a commercial building on the main A.B. Nair Road in Worli. One whole floor above it comprised the office of Shagun.

Mayank hurriedly approached the receptionist. The receptionist, who was busy on phone, had him led by a peon into the conference room. The receptionist's callous behavior only gave credence to whatever perceptions Mayank had begun to form about Revathi and the organization. Perhaps a decadent work culture was the official norm out here, he thought.

As Mayank waited in the conference room, he experienced a strange sinking sort of feeling. He had never before experienced this phenomenon in his career of half a decade. Mayank tried to make light of it by gazing at some posters that adorned the walls of the conference room. They resembled the Kingfisher Calendar that is known to showcase models in rags. They were presumably the print posters of the new beachwear brand that Shagun was launching. And this only confirmed that the rumors to such effect were true.

He imagined a scenario wherein the entire staff of the office were attired in sexy beachwear, just like some of the models used by the brand in its campaign. Better still, he shifted the onus on to Revathi. Though he still didn't have an unambiguous picture of her physical entity, he nonetheless imagined her walking into the conference room attired in an itsy bitsy polka dot bikini just like the poster models. However, almost in the same vein, he attributed this perversion to the effect of being in bad company or more precisely to his association with a weirdo called Vishal. Before he could think any further, the door opened. An attractive thirty something female walked in.

"Hi, I'm Revathi. Revathi Padgaonkar."

Mayank looked at her, mesmerized. Something in his subconscious mind gave him a familiar feel; as if he had met the woman before. He wondered where it could have been.

Revathi truly seemed to have surpassed all his expectations, that is, if he was still left with any. Dressed in an off-white outfit, a salwar and kameez to be precise, she looked demure and pretty. Her eyes were brownish and looked like she had contact lenses on. Her hair, slightly auburn, was smooth, silky and long. She was soft spoken and had a sweet feminine voice that nearly sounded sensuous in this rainy weather.

"I'm sorry I got late," Mayank uttered a bit sheepishly, realizing that his awe of her had him delay the start of conversation.

"It's okay. It must have been tough anyway coming all the way from Andheri in this weather. In fact, if you wanted, I'd have postponed the meeting." Revathi showed the humaneness that was not expected of her.

Mayank was pleasantly surprised at this unexpected warmth. That she mentioned 'Andheri' and correlated it with the massive distance that Mayank must have had to traverse, was by no means borne out of her interest in Geography; instead it had to do with her being a caring woman, he thought. After all, he had mentioned the place just once on the phone when he was asked where the website's office was based.

Even as they exchanged the basic pleasantries before settling down for business, a thought constantly kept Mayank preoccupied. Why did Revathi seem so familiar? Why was he constantly getting the feeling that he had seen her before? Was it a previous birth connection? He hoped not.

Revathi did not waste much time, "So, tell me, Mr. Sahai."

Mayank was about to start when he realized what it was. Revathi was so much like Shweta – the same softness in demeanor, the same warmth, the grace and reassurance. He felt as if he was almost interacting with Shweta after years.

⇐

Mayank made a duly rehearsed presentation, informing Revathi about the website, its reach and how it gelled well with Shagun's target audience. Once he was through, he realized that he had not been interrupted even once, despite problems in concentrating. Rather on one occasion when he had contradicted himself and fumbled, Revathi was supportive enough to ignore it.

Mayank, however, was far from happy with his presentation. He knew he was distracted and why it was so. He'd even finished off his coffee in two huge gulps. He waited nonchalantly for Revathi's reaction.

"Want another cup of coffee?" was all that Revathi said; her tenor strangely protective.

And this only manifested his fears of a goof up. But then why was she being so nice, he wondered. After all, the brand managers he had interacted with were not this kind.

For a moment, an element of doubt surfaced in his mind. He wondered if this act of goodness was for real or if it was a put on. He hadn't come across too many such people of late. Or else, you never know, the lady could be a shrewd flirt. It's extremely difficult to form a conclusive opinion about women, he feared.

However, such notion was quickly dispensed with as Revathi spoke with great authority and command, which in turn reflected her vast knowledge about the work she was dealing in.

"I have a query. Look, we do our own researches and from our findings, almost 4 out of 5 clients who come to our mall, belong to the Sec A and A+ income groups. And in these categories, most marriages are arranged because the families move in the same social circles and know each other. Quite often these marriages are business deals. So I wouldn't know how effective your website will be in reaching out to this category."

Mayank thought for a moment and then put forth a counter argument.

"Well, I agree, ma'am that the class of people you are talking of may not rely so much upon our website. But what our website can do is help you in expanding your customer base. Maybe you might have to price your products differently or maybe introduce a variant line that comes cheaper. Because, I'm sure you realize, ma'am that this market is too huge to be missed out on." Mayank said this with confidence, its resurgence happening at a very opportune moment. Perhaps, Revathi's effect on him had begun to show. Her presence made him feel very comfortable.

Revathi's professionalism was exemplary. She had the ad figures spent by a competing mall and what percentage of these had been apportioned to different media on her fingertips. To his surprise, she was equally well informed about the features of Thematchmaker.com and where it scored or faltered vis-à-vis its competitors. Mayank realized that it made his task somewhat difficult, as he couldn't fool her. Not that he liked fooling people, but then marketing as he had once been advised by one of his seniors was the art of manipulating information so that "cow dung could be sold at the price of gold". He knew he would not be able to do so with Revathi. Perhaps he didn't feel like attempting it either. She was too nice to be maneuvered.

"Ma'am, I must say you've got an amazing bank of information with you," Mayank complimented in awe.

"Oh, thanks. But, trust me; research plays a pivotal part in our work. At least, I'm not the sort who would go solely by gut instincts. The problem with a lot of the young marketing guys these days is that they completely rely on their personality in preparing a sales pitch and in the process negate research. Well, a good personality definitely helps but it's just as important to understand all background info about a product."

Mayank realized that had it been another woman, he'd have even found her didactic, but in Revathi's case, he didn't mind her go on.

The discussion went on. Mayank realized somewhere along that the reason why he kept coming up with interesting arguments to prolong the meeting was perhaps because he just enjoyed listening to Revathi. Her words were pure music to his ears. There was something refreshingly reassuring about her aura. While she looked like a thorough professional to deal with on the work front, she had a rare simplicity about her, which at times even seemed unreal. His concentration remained glued on her eyes and lips as she spoke.

Mayank wondered if Shweta would come across the same way as Revathi, if he were to see her today. There were inescapable similarities in their personalities.

Seven years, however, is a long time; conditions change, experiences change and sometimes people themselves do, he thought. Perhaps, the only aspect of Shweta that he had not seen was that of a professional. She was more homely, even somewhat laidback, coming from a conservative background. Maybe if they'd traversed a longer journey together, she may have transformed and talked the way Revathi did today.

After nearly two hours of discussion, it was time for Revathi to pronounce her verdict. Mayank knew from her positive vibes that he wouldn't go empty handed. The amount of sponsorship, though, he felt wouldn't exceed a couple of lakhs; experience had taught him that a new client essentially looked at brand association before pumping in huge investments. In any case, he felt reasonably excited, as he had always believed that there ought to be face-saving grace even in defeat. Today, even though the website might have to shut, he would still have the satisfaction of having bagged a prestigious client

Revathi finally spelt out what he was dying to hear.

"Well, business is all about taking risks and I guess I'm going to take one today. Unlike other brands that want to be seen all over, I believe in long-term strategic investments. Yes, we'd like to get into a one year deal with you."

Mayank couldn't believe it at first. Nothing had really prepared him for this incredible response, neither the traffic snarls he had to overcome along the way nor the feedback he had been given about the lady. His amazement got the better of him and had him fumble for words.

"Th..th..thank you so much, Ma'am."

Mayank still felt hesitant however to ask Revathi the amount that she would be investing. But she herself chose to dwell on it, as though she could read into what was going on inside Mayank's mind.

"Well as for the amount of the deal, I wouldn't be able to say for sure now. It will depend on the best possible deal that you can work for us."

"Sure Ma'am, I'll mail you a proposal tomorrow itself."

Mayank quickly did his calculations and realized that a worst-case scenario would still get him not less than 10 lac rupees. That added to the existing 3 lacs would total up to over eighty percent of the target given by Ramamurthy.

"Got it! We're through!" Mayank was exclaiming jubilantly in his mind. He knew out of tricks picked along the way that, achieving 80% of the sales target was always safer for a marketing person. Achieving 100% always meant getting the targets raised manifold the next time around.

Mayank was quietly ecstatic. For a moment his face bore an almost blank expression for want of any definite emotion. Relief, ecstasy, gratitude, disbelief had all converged on him in equal measure rendering his speech faculties incoherent for a while. Finally, a wide grin appeared on his face. Revathi wondered what was so strange about her decision so as to make Mayank react in this manner. She had always esteemed the website highly and had only arrived at what she felt was a logically correct decision.

Of course, she had no idea of the resuscitation properties that her decision carried. For Mayank, she had surfaced like an angel and pulled him out of danger almost single-handedly.

Mayank thanked Revathi again and asked for leave, promising to mail her the details ASAP. However, when he looked outside it was clear that the Rain Gods seemed to be having a real field day. Since he had already asked for leave, Mayank felt sheepish prolonging his stay yet again.

"Another cup of coffee?" Revathi smiled.

"Of course," Mayank responded spontaneously, only to check his indulgence the very next moment. "Yeah, I won't mind, if you have time," he said more sedately.

Revathi and Mayank sat over their third cup of coffee. This time their discussion centered round the rain related problems of Mumbai and some suggestions that Revathi made to make thematchmaker.com better. Revathi learnt that Mayank was new to Mumbai. Mayank learnt that Revathi stayed at Lokandwala, which was barely a few hundred meters away from his office. Soon after, the rains ceased and he left.

Till late that evening, celebrations continued at thematchmaker.com. Ramamurthy was in a rare jolly mood. Along with Vishal, he let his hair down to "Kajra re... kajre re..." that played loud on one of the computers. In fact, their spirited effort drew parallels with the performance of Amitabh and Abhishek.

Thereafter, Mayank cut a huge cake. Ramamurthy, in his enthusiasm, went about smearing everybody's face with the cream. It was an unbelievable sight. For, whenever someone had dared to do such a thing in the past, Ramamurthy had blown his vocal chords. Even as everybody exulted, Mayank looked somewhat aloof. Vishal tried probing but he just evaded the issue.

By the time these celebrations got over, it was ten. Vishal's appetite for fun however was not quenched still. He cajoled Mayank and Anil to come out with him on a drive.

They drove across the city roads. With drizzle outside, a bottle of Haywards5000 each in their hands and with a relieving achievement to prod their spirits, life once again looked full of roses. After the initial interaction, Mayank again looked lost. He kept thinking about his meeting with Revathi. After years, someone had come close to resemble "his sort of woman." It took him back into history and into a life he had tried hard to forget.

Vishal drove the car to the Marine Drive, where he finally stopped. Mayank immediately stepped out, all lost by himself and went straight towards the edge of the sea. He looked across the sea to the other side of where Malabar Hills is. Rains had made the entire visual seem mystical; perhaps the positive vibrancy in his thoughts made him feel that much better. Vishal and Anil were, however, not interested in the sight. They probably were not even aware where Mayank was. They were instead watching an MMS that Vishal had saved on his cell. It had Kareena and Shahid smooch each other.

Mayank went and stood atop the small, elevated wall on the edge of the sea. With both his hands stretched outwards, he soaked in every bit of the beauty that the natural ambience carried. In the soft drizzle, his gesture looked so typically romantic. For an onlooker it seemed as if he was striking the Leonardo Di Caprio pose from Titanic. Kate Winslet was conspicuous by her absence, though.

Vishal and Anil, through with their obsession, eventually followed Mayank, wanting to find out what Mayank seemed to be joyfully experiencing in solitude. They couldn't possibly have experienced the same feeling by any chance.

"Hey, I think I've found that perfect woman that I'd been imagining," exclaimed Mayank in sheer joy.

Vishal and Anil looked in surprise. "Wow! And who is she?"

"Revathi."

They were stunned. "You mean the brand manager of Shagun?"

Vishal and Anil gathered that Mayank was already tipsy and perhaps out of his senses. They knew hard beer did not suit him. Mayank, on his part was unfazed and repeated with more clarity.

"Yes, it's her. Revathi Padgaonkar."

4

The First Date

Five days had gone by since the first meeting Mayank had with Revathi; the excitement for the second interface was palpable. The intermittent downpour of the first few days had now made way for light drizzle that would hold on for almost the entire length of the day. The drizzle was so light that one didn't mind actually bathing in it. Driving in it was even more fun.

Apart from the weather, there were two other reasons for the excitement that Mayank felt— one, of course, was to clinch the deal, like it had been prior to the first meeting. The second and more important was simply to meet this woman. Revathi seemed to have had a tantalizing effect on him; the absorbing first interaction had whetted his appetite for a more personalized interaction the second time around. There was a strange inquisitiveness in him to know more about her.

The meeting however had to be postponed as Revathi was supposedly on leave. Mayank wondered what could have been the reason for her going on leave. The last thing he wanted was to know that she had quit her job. After all, on two previous occasions, after making significant inroads in tapping a client, he had to contend with the apocryphal knowledge that 'the concerned person had quit the job and that the new incumbent would review the decision'.

Finally, on Wednesday, Revathi called up out of the blue.

"Actually I've been on leave and hence, have not been coming to office. But since I don't want to put you on hold, I thought I might as well take a couple of hours out and see you this side of the town."

"That'll be great, ma'am,' Mayank nearly jumped in excitement, surprised once again by her unexpected goodness.

"Fine, then, shall we meet at, say, four at the Mocha, Juhu Beach?'

"Yeah, sounds perfect."

"But as far as the release order is concerned, you'll get it only tomorrow"

"Not a problem at all.'

Mayank looked at his watch. It was a quarter to one. The knowledge that in a little over three hours he would be sitting across with Revathi set him up in excitement. He gazed out of the window and felt reassured by the freshness that the drizzle had created all around.

At a half past three, Mayank set off for the venue. He reached the Mocha ten minutes before the scheduled time. This, too, after having significantly de-accelerated his bike speed, once he realized that he was way before time. Revathi had expectedly not arrived yet. Mayank stepped inside and a menu card was soon laid out in front of him.

The menu card listed some beverages that Mayank had only vaguely heard of and most others that sounded completely alien to him. Nonetheless, he didn't want the waiters to get the impression that he'd come there for the first time.

"One Ice Tea," he ordered with reasonable confidence.

Ice Tea was the only beverage he had tasted before.

As Mayank waited for Revathi to arrive, he decided to utilize the time to make sure he was looking good. His physical appearance, after all was something he had always been conscious of. He went inside the rest room.

At 5 feet and 9 inches, Mayank didn't exactly qualify to break into the premium league of 'tall, dark and handsome' men. He, however, didn't fall too short of it either. His soft features, intense eyes, sophisticated demeanor, coupled with his trendy clothes did turn a few heads. The head count would increase on days immediately succeeding a hair cut that made him look really cute. Of late, though, he preferred to keep his hair long.

Another feature that stood out in Mayank's personality was his accented English. It never ceased to surprise his close buddies, who perpetually tried deciphering the source from where this accent was derived. Mayank, after all, had never been abroad. For Mayank, however, it was a carefully crafted device, one that enhanced his suavity manifold and also made people overlook errors in his grammar. Whatever he did, he did with confidence and aplomb. As far as the website was concerned, he was truly 'the most eligible bachelor' in there.

Mayank would normally brace up his unconventional good looks with a pair of macho rectangular sunglasses he had managed to lay his hands on at the Shoppers' Stop after a mammoth search. He would be equally adventurous with his dressing. Unlike his colleagues, who stuck to formal colors, he went for the relatively unexplored ones that included fluorescents on Saturdays. Lest somebody raise an eyebrow over his selection, Mayank made sure that the funkier of his apparels belonged to accepted, up market brands like Provogue and Tuscan Verve. Today, however, he wore a neat white shirt with maroon stripes and complemented it with formal black trousers.

It was almost a quarter past four and Revathi was still not there. Mayank wondered where she'd have been held up. He tried guessing which car she used. His gut instinct was that it would be a Hyundai Accent. He didn't know how he arrived at it though. Mayank sipped the ice tea, looking almost every few seconds at his watch. He wondered what was wrong with the 'timing' this time.

Right then, Mayank saw an auto arrive outside the Mocha. From the white salwar clad legs that were visible to him from where he sat, he knew the passenger was a female. When the female stepped out, carrying an umbrella, he realized, to his surprise that it was Revathi. Over her white salwar she wore an orange kameej. The kameej reached a little above her knees– her thighs to be more precise. And from the transparency of the chiffon white that was more apparent in its wet form, Mayank could make out she had great pair of legs. She was sporting a neat pair of black, rimmed glasses that confirmed that the other day her brown eyeballs were indeed contact lenses. Her long hair was neatly assembled and clipped behind. Her countenance wore a preoccupied expression from which Mayank could make out that she was perhaps just that wee bit busy and wouldn't have much time to spare.

For a moment, the sight took him into nostalgia and he recounted a September afternoon when Shweta and he walked down the University Campus in one of Delhi's rare thundershowers. The heavy rains had both of them scurrying under one umbrella. The intensity of the rains was such that they virtually clung together. He had never since seen a woman look so beautiful in the rains.

Mayank wondered why the long-forgotten image suddenly resurfaced in his mind. He surmised that it had to do with the vulnerable expression on Revathi's countenance. Shweta had looked just as vulnerable that afternoon. And Mayank had proposed to her on the spur of the moment.

"Hey, I'm sorry for the delay. My chauffeur just didn't turn up," Revathi apologized as she approached Mayank's table.

"No issues, Ma'am."

Mayank felt a little awkward realizing that his ice tea was almost over. "What would you have?"

Revathi thought for a moment. "Costa Rica Tarrazu."

Mayank was really confused. He couldn't exactly make out her words.

"Yeah, I'll go for Costa Rica Tarrazu."

Her reiteration gave him a slightly clearer idea that what she uttered was a coffee type. He did not want to risk pronouncing it though. The safer alternative, therefore, was to call the waiter.

"I understand you've been on leave these last few days. Anything serious?" queried Mayank, meaning to come across as being concerned.

"No, nothing serious as such. Just that my daughter, Ria has her exams and during exams she really goes crazy without me. So I thought I might as well spend some time with her and help her out."

For a moment, Mayank was absolutely clueless on how to react. Revathi's physical appearance did not hide the fact that she was reasonably older to him. If Mayank was on the verge of marriage, logically it was only correct to believe that Revathi would be married and possibly have children too. But somehow the mention of her daughter seemed to have taken him off guard. It was like he was told something he had been wishing not to hear.

"How old is your daughter?' asked Mayank, putting the shock aside and intending to take the conversation ahead.

"Well, Ria is eight. She's in Standard Three. Besides, you know these rains can be a real pain if they go on and on."

Mayank realized that Revathi sounded rather digressive; perhaps she was physically there but her mind was elsewhere. He empathized with her, for he realized that managing the dual roles in office and home must be difficult.

Revathi, then, took out a large size envelope and gave it to Mayank.

"I went through your proposal and also discussed it with my boss. We've decided to invest 12 lacs on the annual deal, wherein thematchmaker.com would provide us a regular banner on the home page and connectivity to our site."

Mayank couldn't believe his ears when he heard this. Surely his joy was boundless.

"Thanks a ton, Ma'am. I promise we'll go all out to promote your brand."

Revathi's magnanimity instantly increased their comfort levels manifold. Within minutes, their conversation extended beyond work related issues. Mayank, for his part, tried to quench his inquisitiveness by extracting more from her on her personal front.

"So are you from Mumbai?

"No, I'm basically from Delhi. I've been here for the last 10 years now."

Mayank realized that Revathi did not speak about her husband. A flurry of myriad thoughts came into his mind on this count. Is her marriage on? Why does she have to worry so much about the kid when the husband could also help her out? Or is she just too selfless to allow her husband to be burdened unnecessarily? Whatever it must have been, Mayank did not want to talk about her husband – he had, with experience, realized that when one wanted to flirt with a married woman, nothing could be more dampening than allowing the woman to speak about her husband-good or bad.

Revathi looked quite relaxed as the interaction progressed.

"So how do you find Mumbai? These rains must be unnerving for someone who is not used to it."

"No, on the contrary, I've begun to like Mumbai a little more in the last five days, ever since we met."

Revathi was a little taken aback by the utterance of the last four words that Mayank spoke and Mayank was quick to realize it. He quickly covered up by saying. "Well, I mean that was the first day of the rains."

Mayank, thereafter, flowed with the tide, providing Revathi with interesting topical cues from where she picked up the conversation. He knew from experience that nothing was more important for a marketing person than a personal rapport with the client.

"You know something you're different from other marketing people. Hardcore sales people don't talk weather or the city. I mean they try to but more often than not, their superficiality gets exposed. You come across as a more sensitive being."

Mayank was quite surprised by the compliment. He, however, didn't quite know the significance of what she had said. Did she really find him so impressive? Or was she, by any means trying to hint that he was not a competent marketing professional? Given that Revathi would be meeting so many marketing people she would surely be able to tell the good ones from the bad. Mayank, himself believed that good human beings often did not make successful professionals. Or was it a very natural observation she had made? In any case, her statement reflected a certain dislike for the ways of typical marketing professionals and that was surprising given she herself was one.

"Ma'am, you're also different from the other brand managers that I've met. You come across as a very warm and nice person. I mean one would not see too many brand managers talking to media sellers with such warmth and reception like you do."

"I guess that must have to do something with my Psychology background. I find it interesting to interact with different people and try to figure out why a person behaves in a certain manner."

"Ah, I guess I ought to be more careful. I'm sure, you'd be trying to figure out something about me also as we talk?"

"Not really. But what I find interesting in you is the vulnerability of an ambitious youngster who comes down to Mumbai with certain aspirations and who is trying hard to stick to those aspirations. You know what -the interesting thing about this city is that it often has a very different agenda for you than what your own aspiration is."

Mayank wondered if it was her knowledge of Psychology that made her speak with such precision or if she really found him an interesting being to think of.

"Ma'am, but how come you came into advertising after Psychology?"

"I guess if I had to take the decision today, I'd have gone for my Masters in Psychology itself. But, in our days, we would more often than not do what our elders in the house wanted us to. My Mom got me the forms for this institute. I filled it up and the rest just followed."

"Is there any particular person whose life has interested you the most? Or do you try to find interesting aspects in various people."

"Women interest me. If it were possible for me I would love to get into the minds of a few women and really unravel their psyche."

"And who would these women be?"

"I wouldn't know for sure. But women who've been in unusual situations and whose lives have had more happening in them than what your and my life can ever accommodate."

"Women like…"

"Well, a Sonia Gandhi for sure, maybe Rabri Devi. If I go down the list further maybe a Phoolan Devi if she were alive, maybe even a Mallika Sherawat."

"But why these women if I may ask?"

"Because they are all survivors. From fragile beginnings, they all went on to attain a position where they simply couldn't be wished away. "

Revathi seemed to be in a nearly didactic mode and went on.

"Besides, you know what, it's very easy to paint people in white or black. But life is really not that simple. I personally feel that we cannot judge people unless we step into their shoes and unless we really understand their psyche," she explained.

From the passion with which Revathi spoke, Mayank could sense her feel vicariously for these women. It also emboldened him to make queries, some even a bit personal in nature. Revathi answered freely, which only meant that she was comfortable opening up in front of him. Mayank gathered that she was fascinated to know and understand the human mind.

"In fact, I wish I could be five different people in one life. Life is so boring being just what you are, nah?"

49

Mayank couldn't agree more. After all, he himself had always wanted so much more out of life than the stipulated framework within which his life was confined. And then Revathi uttered something that quite took Mayank by surprise.

"You know something. In my previous life, I was a Hindu minister in the durbar of Razia Sultan."

Mayank looked stunned by this sudden shift to the surreal. But Revathi continued undaunted and with the same conviction.

"I was stabbed to death on my back by some envious courtier. Even today, I experience a sudden pain at times at a particular portion on my back and I've found out it has a karmic connection…"

Revathi then explained that this was told to her by a spiritual guru whom she had visited in Trivandrum and who claimed to be a 'past life therapist'. This person could tell what a person was in his or her previous life merely by examining the person's forehead. She also revealed that later her curiosity had led her to undergo a couple of therapy sessions by a Mumbai based expert who actually made her relive certain moments from her previous life wherein she spoke a completely alien language; that too in a virtually unimaginable manly voice. She could also visualize a clear picture of the colossal durbar. Revathi informed that she was however forced to quit these sessions abruptly as they resulted in her experiencing delusions. She found it disturbing her present life.

"But why did you go for it in the first place?" Mayank asked in confusion.

"I guess it was just curiosity. It was a quest to discover life beyond its tangible form. Besides the inquisitiveness to experience being one more entity."

Mayank's shock remained unabated. He was almost speechless

for a while. He gathered that perhaps beneath Revathi's calm exterior, she had a knack for wild adventure. Besides she must be really gutsy. At least, Mayank was pretty convinced he didn't have the courage to rake up his past life.

The interaction had whetted Mayank's interest even more. From giving him food for thought on numerous issues to even dealing a sudden scare, Revathi's conversation had given him all in the last few minutes. She truly came across as one hell of an interesting person to know, he thought. Like him she had the ability to spring surprises aplenty.

Mayank decided to go for another coffee. He called the waiter.

"Get me one Costa Rica Tarazu."

Revathi was surprised at the choice. Mayank, however, sounded pretty sure. He wanted to experience the magic the coffee had done to Revathi's spirit.

"So where do you see yourself heading in life, say five years hence?" asked Revathi.

"I have no idea".

"What?'

"Yes, I am essentially a dreamer. In my school days I wanted to be a cricketer. Then, at one stage when I realized that that won't be possible, I wanted to attempt the civil services."

"But cricket and civil services are so different."

"Yes, but I guess, power and fame is what always attracted me and both these professions stock them in good measure."

"Then what happened?"

"Then when I realized that even that won't happen, I did what all my friends were doing. I did my MBA and started working. But I still want to do a lot of things…"

51

"Hmmm… Interesting! But frankly, you don't sound like someone that confused."

"Actually the problem with me is that all my life I've done things to prove a point to others… and to myself. In the process, I never got to know what really my strengths are and what I ought to do."

Revathi looked impressed by this naked honesty.

"But do you have any picture of where you see your life culminating eventually?"

Mayank took a long pause. He almost weighed the repercussions of what he was going to say before he finally spoke.

"Yeah… Well, I want to be the Prime Minister of the country."

Mayank's words almost carried a juvenile streak in it. Revathi was beginning to realize that Mayank had this propensity to make some really far-reaching statements with a near straight jaw. She wouldn't know when he was serious and when he would be joking. But her doubts were soon enough allayed.

Mayank spoke about his interest in politics with amazing clarity.

"I really don't understand why people react in such a shocked way when someone talks about his interest in politics. I mean is it that bad? Look, even our freedom struggle was purely a political movement. If you go back and examine the petty politicking that different leaders resorted to against each other even then, you would be shocked. Yet the movement gave us the gift of freedom. Besides, to fight the system, you first have to be a part of the system."

Revathi heard him out.

"Besides, isn't there enough politics happening at our workplaces anyway?"

What impressed Revathi all the more was the ideological

conviction behind his thought. He was also quite unequivocal about his 'Rightist' moorings.

Both Mayank and Revathi were beginning to discover their abilities to stun, to be unpredictable; and to be so with rare conviction. This was an endearing feature not everybody could boast of.

They soon realized that their coffees had been over for sometime. They'd been instead sipping the magic of their interaction.

"You know my mother always used to tell me that the more you chase something, the further it goes away from you. And when you stop chasing it, if it's destined, it does come back to you. At least I've found it true in my life." Revathi philosophized, still thinking about Mayank's maverick aspirations.

The conversation got as interesting as it could get. In no time Mayank and Revathi had spent two hours chatting, of which only a miniscule portion had to do with the business that had brought him there.

"Gosh! It's almost six. I'll have to go as my daughter will be back from her tuitions," Revathi said finally. In an instant afterthought she added, "I don't think there is much to discuss about the deal, since we're sticking to the Plan B you had mailed to us. As far as the release order is concerned, we'll issue that in a couple of days."

"Sure."

Mayank looked lost. The conversation had been far too engrossing to come out of it instantly. Besides the reassuring aura, the refreshing beauty and the wealth of fascinating knowledge of the person he had spent the last two hours with was rubbing on him.

The waiter brought the bill for them. It was for an amount of Rs. 240. Mayank made a beeline for it, intending to pay. Revathi on the other hand would not let him do.

"Ma'am, but it's my treat. You don't know how important this deal is for us."

"But the call was mine, right?"

They had a minor skirmish on who would pay. Revathi however worked it out.

"Okay, we'd rather share. But I'll pay Rs.160."

"But that's not sharing."

"That is. Don't forget I'm older to you. Besides, you must save up money from now if you want to enter the uncertain world of politics."

Revathi's mild-mannered pulling of Mayank's legs instantly let off the tension. What did not escape Mayank's observation, however, was Revathi's protective tenor when she spoke of her being older to him.

"But how did you arrive at the figure of 160?"

"Well, that's two thirds of the total amount. So if we ever have coffee together again, I'll be your two-thirds partner." She smiled.

Mayank wondered if there was a method to her craziness. After all, she had made him her one-third partner so effortlessly.

Then, almost immediately, she digressed into sounding rather romantic. "You know, these drizzles invariably have fond memories for all of us. When I first **met** Pranav, it was raining exactly like this."

"Pranav?"

"Yeah, my husband."

Mayank's smile faded away. He realized that for some strange reason, he was already feeling possessive about the woman. He had no clue why it was so.

Later that night, when Mayank thought about the meeting in hindsight, he realized that it was a date, he'd not have imagined. Most of the things that they'd ended up discussing sounded abstract. Yet, the pleasure he derived from thinking about the meeting was almost orgasmic.

It had been a date, he was sure, he'd remember in a long time. He wanted to meet Revathi again. And meet her soon. He wondered how that could be.

Next morning when Mayank reached office, he went straight to Vishal.

"Vishal, you'll have to do me a favor."

"What?"

"You'll have to do a story on Revathi."

Vishal was confused at the abruptness of the request.

"Don't say no and don't ask me why, just plan it out somehow. You'll have to do this for me."

Vishal knew why but did not know how to justify it. Both thought hard when Mayank suddenly erupted with an idea.

"Do a story under the segment 'Couple of the Fortnight'."

Vishal was yet to react when Mayank added, "Call it A HAPPY FAMILY."

5

A Happy Family

Revathi was still asleep when she felt a caressing sensation on her cheeks. A few indulgent fingers carefully set aside the strands of hair that had straggled onto Revathi's face, hampering a clear view of her countenance; its innocence looked enhanced manifold in the ignorance of slumber. It was a sight that seemed to have some form of addictive powers for Pranav. Pranav simply relished it and what followed was a series of soft, wet pecks in the vicinity of her lips.

Over the last few years, Revathi had got so accustomed to this ritual that no sooner would the act begin, she would in her subconscious mind start awaiting the finale. The first kiss would be followed within a few seconds by a second, one on either cheek. It, in some way, had come to be an alarm bell for her, indicating that it was about 7 in the morning. And if the second was not sufficient to wake her up, a third would follow. Only on the third kiss, Pranav made sure he rubbed his stubble real hard on Revathi's face; for the moment it happened, she would get up with a jerk, livid at Pranav. As if to compensate for it, Pranav would then bring about the crescendo- a lip lock, a true blue tongue twisting that Revathi thoroughly enjoyed and which in some way prepared her for the long hours of separation during the day.

Over a period of time, Revathi had actually started enjoying the rubbing of Pranav's stubble the most, because it was the precursor to something really fabulous. Though it inflicted some amount of pain, it was a pain she willingly absorbed, ensconced in the reassurance of the magical relief she knew would synonymously follow.

However, today as Pranav's fingers got into the act, he experienced a sudden spurt that propelled him to skip some of the chores. He ended up directly kissing his wife's lips instead. Revathi woke up at once. She looked into Pranav's eyes, wanting to decipher the cause of that extra glint.

"Happy Anniversary darling; today, our marriage completes a decade," beamed Pranav.

"To you, too, sweetheart."

They hugged and felt each other passionately for almost a minute, just the way they had done after making love for the first time.

However, soon after, Pranav wound up the act rather abruptly. He got up suddenly to start off with the normal, routine activities; his suddenness made him appear even phlegmatic. A strange sort of abruptness had crept into Pranav's behavior lately. Though Revathi found it a little weird at times, she realized what was causing it. The last two years had been bad for Pranav professionally.

Revathi, however, gave in to inertia. She lingered on in bed for a while. She tried to feel the importance of the day; a decade of successful married life, after all meant a lot in these times. The ambience seemed just about right for her to slip into nostalgia.

Revathi had seen her parents go through an acrimonious marriage before her father passed away when she was barely ten. She had grown up since, viewing marriages with skepticism. Her role model was her mother, Rohini Tiwari. Both Revathi and her younger sister, Rupali doted on her. A senior political journalist with the Hindustan Times, Rohini had put her personal trauma aside to excel in her profession. Rohini's influence had, at some point, sunk into Revathi's subconscious mind and led her to believe a man was unnecessary in a woman's existence. A family, she thought, was complete without men.

It was when Revathi was around nineteen and in the first year of her degree course at Indraprastha College that her belief got shaken. Her mother Rohini was linked with a powerful politician, Saurabh Dikshit.

Saurabh was the one of the most influential of the second rung leaders of Indian Peoples Party that had only recently come to power. Known to have a taste for the good things in life he was just as selective about women. The one known case of his dalliance outside marriage was with a female IFS officer, who was serving the External Affairs Ministry, which he served as Minister of State six years ago. And now it was Rohini. It was rumored that these reports were actually planted in the media by rivals within his party. Little of course, would they have known of the morbid repercussions that it would cause in an apolitical family grappling with its own set of trials and tribulations.

On a chilly winter night of January, when the mercury must have dipped to its lowest, Rohini confessed to her elder daughter of having been in a relationship with Saurabh. She had done so hoping that Revathi was big enough to understand her position; and perhaps that she must know the truth. But when Revathi first heard it, the shock of it almost numbed the impact of the cold. Her faith had indeed been devastated.

The confession led to the mother and daughter drifting apart; Revathi would always nurse a grouse against her mother. Perhaps Revathi's puritanical moorings had led her to paint everything in white or black; it certainly had not in the remotest way prepared her to accept the reality of a forty something single woman's emotional needs.

≈

Nearly three years later, Revathi was doing her Post Graduate Diploma in Advertising and it was yet another chilly wintry January evening. Dressed in two thick cardigans that covered her till the neck, Revathi, along with about a score of other students waited in her class for Pranav Padgaonkar.

Pranav, a renowned Mumbai-based ad-film maker was supposed to take a guest lecture. He arrived about half an hour late and blamed it conveniently on the weather that had led to his flight from Mumbai getting delayed.

Surprisingly, Pranav did not look like anyone would have expected him to. Revathi felt that for someone that successful, he was remarkably young and also good looking. He was fair, about 5 feet and 10 inches tall, had intense eyes embedded neatly between his soft features. He had the kind of personality that made the female students look up at him attentively. The two things Revathi didn't like about him were his beard and the ponytail, which she found rather stale. Even as Pranav taught, she viewed him quite intently; there was something in his personality that stood out and drew attention. Perhaps, she thought it was the freshness of unconventional good looks, coupled with rare sophistication and intellect, a combination she hadn't come across too often among Delhi's Punju brigade. For Delhi men, she believed, looking good was all about being macho, although she quite dreaded even the handsomest of them opening their mouths.

Pranav apparently got conscious of Revathi constantly looking at him; in a rather clichéd retort, he directed almost all of his revision questions at her. Revathi barely managed to answer half of them.

"Next time, you better be more attentive," Pranav had signed off with a mischievous smile. Revathi hated him for this

Exactly four months later, summer was at its peak in Mumbai when Revathi was called for an interview in an Advertising Agency. Five other students from her institute were also called. The girls put up at a hostel on Bandra's Hill Road; the two boys took a lodge in Dadar. Humidity must have been at its worst at that time, but Revathi was not complaining. Delhi had begun to bore her. The awkwardness that had crept into her relationship with her mother had led to disillusionment. Her younger sister and she weren't the best of confidants either. Besides, the same rigmarole of politicians, government employees, political journalists and DTC buses had made Revathi want to break out of the city. In her heart of hearts, when she boarded the Mumbai bound train, she had hoped that Mumbai would somehow 'absorb' her.

Pranav, incidentally, happened to be on the panel that interviewed the students. Revathi thought it to be a coincidence. The interview, however, was bad to say the least; apart from Pranav, who appeared reasonable, the three other members were nearly hostile for unknown reasons. That very evening, the results were out and none got selected.

Revathi spent the evening gazing blankly at the sea at Bandstand. Mumbai appeared tantalizing in the glitter of the evening lights. Besides, the hub of business was also the hub of free expression of love; she thought. What else could have explained couples uninhibitedly expressing their feelings for each other– some behind rocks and others in full public view? And to think of it, there were a couple of same sex couples as well. One thing that Revathi instantly admired about the city was its sovereign culture, a near infallible 'live and let live' attitude— something she had longed for in Delhi.

Revathi felt defeated that night when she returned to the hostel. She knew that next afternoon when she would board the Paschim Express back to Delhi, she will have completely lost out on an opportunity to work and be in the city of her dreams.

Next afternoon, Revathi waited at a platform on Mumbai Central while the two male students in the group ran around trying to confirm the reservation. The station was particularly crowded that day; there were people returning after having spent their holidays in Mumbai, then there were others who were pouring in for admissions to undergraduate courses in the city's colleges.

In this incessant hullabaloo, Revathi was surprised to spot a familiar face. She saw the 'familiar' person surge in towards the coach outside which she stood. The person was frantically searching for his coach; to her disbelief it was none other than Pranav. Pranav hadn't yet seen her when she called him from behind.

"Sir. Excuse me, sir."

Pranav turned and looked both shaken and relieved.

"What's the matter, Sir? Are you traveling by this train?"

"Yeah, nnnno. No. Actually, I was looking for someone."

Revathi thought it must have been his wife.

"Actually, I was looking for you."

Revathi was thoroughly surprised to hear this before Pranav explained the situation.

"Well, an agency called Maa Bozell, for whom I'm shooting an ad film, is looking for an Account Trainee. I read your resume and thought you fitted the requirement. I had called up the number mentioned on your resume, only to be told that you had left for the station. I thought I'd come straight to the station...."

Revathi was surprised at the effort that Pranav had made for her. She was just as confused.

"But what do I do now?' Revathi asked with the vulnerability of a school kid who had lost her way.

"Well..."

By this time, her friends had joined the debate.

"But it isn't a job offer, right? From what I understand there is just a vacancy," reasoned one of Revathi's friends.

"No, no, it's a job. I mean it's as good as one. The CEO of the firm is well known to me and I had forwarded all your resumes to him. He liked Revathi's profile and selected her. In fact, she could be needed to join ASAP," asserted Pranav.

The train was to depart in the next five minutes. The group appeared undecided still. Sensing that the advantage of his age and experience would make the youngsters heed to him, Pranav tried drilling in a solution.

"Look if I were in your place, I wouldn't miss out on this opportunity. In fact the only reason I've made this effort for you is because as a teacher I want that you should get the best."

His last sentence almost reeked of desperation, though Revathi didn't sense it.

A few minutes later, the train left. And Mumbai indeed seemed to have answered Revathi's call. It had 'absorbed' her. What Revathi did not realize, though, was that her life was now out of the realm of sheer destiny; someone had laid a plan on it. She went back to stay in the same hostel and joined the ad agency the next day. Revathi's decision shocked Rohini initially but she stood by her daughter and even promised to come down to see her within a month. Pranav now enjoyed the position of a respected mentor to her, someone she could really look up to.

A week went by in getting accustomed to the new routine in the new place. Traveling in jam-packed local trains from Bandra to Churchgate and then taking a bus to Colaba was more painstaking than taking a DTC bus from Mayur Vihar to ITO. And yet Revathi was not complaining. Mumbai had toughened her, she thought. In her rookie eagerness to meet deadlines religiously, she had already once stayed back in office till midnight. And yet when she returned to her hostel at 1 in the night, she did not feel any fear on the way. She realized that such a thing would not have been possible in Delhi. Delhi was notorious for its lack of security for women. One had even heard stories of the staff on late night buses plying in the outer regions molesting female passengers.

It was a Friday evening. The monsoon was round the corner. It had been cloudy throughout the day. Besides, the second Saturday of the month, being a holiday, the weekend ambience had already set in. This resulted in a let up in concentration and made Revathi feel homesick. In those moments, she got a call from Pranav on the office number.

"Hi, how have you been?'

"Oh, good, sir. Thanks. How about you?"

"Well, I'd come to The Taj for a meeting. I'm through now and going back. I just thought I'd find out your work situation. If you are through, maybe we could meet for coffee and then I can drop you to your hostel."

Pranav's call couldn't have come at a more opportune moment. As Revathi had been feeling low, she just jumped at the prospect.

Half an hour later, they sat over coffee at a Café outside Churchgate station. By this time, it had become really windy; the weather seemed almost adventurously romantic. Sensing Pranav's soft corner for her, Revathi had begun to feel inquisitive about him.

"So have you been in Mumbai throughout?"

"Yep. All my 29 years."

Pranav appeared distracted by the weather.

"This weather is so romantic, just the kind when you would want to take a drive to Lonavala with your girlfriend." He added with a tinge of disappointment. "Unfortunately, I don't have one."

"Isn't it a little surprising that a successful, handsome person like you is still single?" Revathi nearly stunned herself with this daring personal query. For a moment, she even got a feeling that Pranav was leading her up to the point where she would probe him. She however didn't give it a serious thought.

"Yes, surprising it is. You know our country is facing an acute problem of the falling sex ratio of females. I guess that is what has done me in. Good girls just aren't there."

Pranav did have a sense of humor, even if it was bizarre, she thought.

"But lately I think I have spotted someone. I'm just too scared to propose to her."

The meeting had to be curtailed midway as the anticipation of thundershowers had people scurrying in near frenzy. The weather department, it seemed had predicted very heavy downpour.

Pranav and Revathi had barely traveled about a third of the distance in Pranav's Fiat when it started pouring. Within moments, they encountered quite a huge traffic jam in the road alongside Haji Ali on the Worli Seaface. Left stranded in an unusual situation, Pranav checked out for the audio cassettes he had. There was only one, of the film SAAJAN, with Sanjay Dutt looking rather pathetically at them, limping. Pranav sheepishly asked if he could play the cassette. He had no idea then that Revathi had no interest in English Songs. The songs started playing in low volume.

It was actually quite an unusual situation for both. It was the first time that they had met informally and the weather Gods had already been unkind. Pranav attempted to make light of the situation by cracking a few sardarji jokes. The effort was so contrived that Revathi could sense it. Nonetheless, she made an effort to laugh. She didn't know, however, if the laugh was meant for the jokes or Pranav's effort. She contrasted this nervous looking Pranav from the reassured one she had first seen in her institute. Something was surely amiss; she did not know what.

A few minutes later, traffic seemed to have cleared somewhat; the vehicles in front had begun to move. In another minute or so, they too were likely to move.

"What is the craziest thing you've done in your life?" Pranav asked abruptly.

"Hmmmm. Let me think. Well, once I slipped out of my class right under my cock-eyed Professor's nose after he had taken the attendance."

"That's not crazy."

"Yeah? What's your craziest deed been then?"

"Well, I'm going to do that now."

Revathi wondered what Pranav was up to.

"I'm going to ask you a difficult question."

Even this caveat did not prepare Revathi for what was coming.

"Will you marry me?"

Before she could answer, the traffic cleared and Pranav had to concentrate in getting through the dense clutter of vehicles. The question kept ringing in her ears. She even wondered once if she was hallucinating. But there was a reminder that made her feel doubly certain she was not.

"Did you hear me? I said, 'will you marry me?'"

The song that played on the car stereo at that moment almost seemed to reinforce Pranav's state of mind.... *Mera dil bhi kitna paagal hai, yeh pyar to tum se karta hai....*

Revathi found herself in a very unusual situation. Experiencing the season's first rains from the ensconced shelter of a car plying right in the middle of the road and with someone to drive it was quite an experience in itself; on top of it she had been proposed to in life for the first time, that too by an incredibly eligible bachelor. Her ecstasy in fact made her feel nervous, as she had not quite known life to be that kind. Her nervousness made her procrastinate. Revathi, eventually, warded off the question rather coyly.

"By when do you think I can get back to you on this?" she asked looking as cute as a summer trainee who had no idea of what the assignment required. Pranav was quite amused by this response. He felt surer and more reassured that she had no prior experience of romance.

That night, Revathi painted images of living together with

hubby Pranav in her mind. Fortunately for her, Pranav's pony tail was now gone. How would a bearded husband look like, she tried visualizing. Revathi felt confident that she would make him shave it off, maybe put that as a condition before agreeing for marriage. In some corner of her mind there was this apprehension though, that Pranav may not be genuine and that perhaps he enjoyed flirting around with girls. But a near spontaneous counter analysis concluded that asking for marriage was way beyond flirting. Besides he did care for her and had proved it so.

Excitement kept Revathi awake till the wee hours of the morning.

Next morning, Revathi woke up late and began the day reading the newspaper. It had been raining heavily and so it was indeed such a relief that she didn't have to go to office. At around a half past ten, she was told that there was a call for her and that she must go to the reception as the person will call again in the next five minutes. She thought it must be her Mom worried over the TV reports announcing that normal life had been paralyzed in Mumbai due to rains.

To her surprise, the caller was Pranav.

"Good morning. I thought I should find out your decision. And if you haven't been able to take one, if I may help you out with it.'

Revathi was still sleepy and did not know whether accepting over the phone would really be that romantic. After all, in the last twelve hours, she had begun to feel like she was falling in love—the first time so.

'Actually… can we meet and talk?'

"Yes, of course, how about a dinner tonight at Gazebo on the Linking Road?"

By the time they met for dinner, the heavy downpour had given way to a mild drizzle. Mumbai, in its wetness seemed more alluring than ever, more so, in anticipation of the interaction that was to happen. Since the rains had kept most people at home, the restaurant was only half full and this made Revathi feel slightly less nervous. It was time finally for Revathi to shoot.

"Well, I don't really know what to say. I am flattered that of all girls you must be meeting regularly, you found interest in me. May I ask you what interested you about me so much?"

Pranav thought.

"Well, let me see if I have an answer. I guess you appear very pristine; there is something very mystical about your persona. Besides when one has to take important decisions like this, one always tends to go for substance. You are more like what my mother was, my sister is and what I would want my daughter to be like."

Revathi felt overwhelmed by this last bit that Pranav said. By now, she was well and truly in love.

"I can't possibly say no. Yes, I'll marry you."

Pranav confessed later that he had taken a fancy for her the very first time he saw her. Her eyes exuded a rare sincerity, something he hadn't seen in other girls. On knowing her, he was glad that the eyes reflected the person she was.

A couple of weeks later in the wee hours of a Tuesday, Pranav made Revathi walk down to the Siddhivinayak Temple from her hostel in Bandra. The march took about two hours and they reached the temple in time for the first Aarti of Tuesday morning. Even as they walked down, Revathi was quite surprised to see dozens of other people doing the same. Pranav explained later that the ritual was considered auspicious; his mother would follow it religiously at least once every year till she was alive and that he just wanted to keep the tradition going. For Revathi, the walk revived faint memories of walking up to the Vaishno Devi more than a decade and half ago, perhaps the last time she had traveled with her father.

Revathi and Pranav prayed for happiness.

About a year later, they got married in Delhi. True to the ways of the glitterati in Delhi, the marriage took place at a Gurgaon farmhouse. Among those who blessed the couple was Saurabh Dikshit, who had become the Civil Aviation Minister. When Saurabh blessed the couple, Rohini looked into her daughter's eyes with guilt. Her daughter, strangely, had empathy for her. Perhaps finding her own true love had softened Revathi and made her understand the emotional needs of her single mother. Besides, the way Rohini had supported Revathi in her relationship with Pranav, had possibly eroded whatever angst she may have had for Rohini.

The couple went on a honeymoon to the UK, Revathi's first trip abroad. However, the honeymoon continued till much after their return. A year after their marriage Pranav won the RAPA award for the best Ad-film director. He, without a doubt, dedicated it to his lovely wife, "who had transformed his life and brought out the best in him". In a short span, Revathi rose to being the Account Manager in her advertising agency. It was when the couple was holidaying in the Kerala backwaters that Revathi learnt that she was carrying. Pranav celebrated the news by giving her a very special massage on a secluded beach. A few months later, Ria was born. Two years into the marriage, the couple had every reason to believe that they were the best thing to have happened to each other.

PART II

T he euphoria of the early post marriage phase continued for the next few years. And perhaps could have continued longer. However, something or the other had been going amiss in the last couple of years.

Pranav had virtually reached a stage of stagnancy as far as his work was concerned. Shooting ad films no longer excited him, what with newer kids ruling the roost. For one year, he virtually sat home, trying to figure out what to do, before his old friend and colleague, Sonal landed back in India.

Sonal, had at one point, assisted Pranav in directing ad films in the early part of his career. She had a boyfriend at that point, with whom she was going through a rough patch. And Sonal never quite let go of an opportunity to send feelers to Pranav on whom she had a massive crush. Pranav, for his part, definitely found Sonal sexy, even though he wasn't particularly fond of women with short hair. But despite her repeated efforts, he never felt convinced that they could really go beyond a one night stand. And as a policy, Pranav avoided one night stands with women he was working with, for he had learnt from experience how complicated they could be.

Sonal's problems with her boyfriend only grew. And then one night, she suddenly disappeared. A few weeks later, a close female friend of hers informed that Sonal was in the States. Nothing was heard from her end for years thereafter, till she returned a couple of years ago.

Sonal came back with another man, Kirti Patel, an Indian born painter, born and brought up in New Jersey. They had been in a live in relationship for a while. Once back, she tried connecting with old friends and acquaintances. However, a couple of months after coming down, she suffered a jolt when Kirti got afflicted by some mysterious ailment and died. Rumors had it that he was HIV positive, something Sonal denied vehemently. Kirti's death, however, left Sonal in a traumatized state.

Sonal then turned to Pranav for support. And as a good human being, Pranav provided so, in good measure. Soon enough, they decided to float a software production company together.

Sonal was different from Revathi in several obvious ways. When Revathi would look at her, she would be instantly reminded of how Pranav himself described such women- *they could be friends, not wives.* Revathi wondered in that case what made Pranav get along with Sonal so well.

Revathi, despite being an unprejudiced person, had this rare intuitive quality in her that made her beware of certain people. And Sonal happened to be one such person whose presence created unusual negative vibes in her. When Pranav first informed her about the decision to start a production company with Sonal, Revathi was shocked.

"But Pranav, why do you need an association with Sonal? She has been away for years. How would she know what works over here and what does not?"

"Yeah, I know Sonal isn't too much in sync with the Indian industry, but then she is a quick learner. What she lacks by experience, she more than makes up with her zest and passion."

"Well, it's your decision. I just thought I should tell you to think it over once more."

"Hey, hey, Revathi, are you feeling jealous?"

Revathi wasn't the least bit amused. She ignored him. Her ignoring him spelt out her disapproval more prominently.

Sonal came across as a supremely confident and haughty woman, so much so that it sometimes made her appear insolent. She smoked like a chimney. Her body language was replete with physicality; hugging a male colleague or patting him on his cheek came easy to her. Moreover, she had a childish, possessive streak in her, which when it manifested itself, made her reasoning go for a toss. Hence, when Pranav, once forgot to call her back, Sonal assumed that Revathi had prevented him from doing so and instead asked him to end their business venture, there and then. This behavior, entirely unprovoked, revealed her insecurities. Revathi suspected that Sonal still lusted for Pranav. But Pranav would just laugh it off whenever Revathi made such a suggestion.

In the last few weeks however, Sonal and Pranav's proximity had only grown. This had to do with Sony TV having expressed an interest in one of the concepts for a daily soap that they narrated to it. The hope of actually being able to put their first show on air made them work that much harder. And since they didn't still have an office of their own, Pranav and Sonal would alternately operate from each other's home. Revathi didn't like this one bit, but chose to give her husband "space".

Revathi walked into her office one day and was greeted warmly by her colleague, Prabhakar.

"Hey, I didn't know our tastes were so similar," teased Prabhakar.

Revathi had no clue in what context Prabhabar said this.

"So how was dinner at the Copper Chimney?"

"Copper Chimney?"

"Yeah. Didn't Pranav tell you? "

"What? "

"Well, my wife and I were stepping out of the Copper Chimney last night, when we bumped into Pranav and Sonal, who were walking in. They were perhaps coming from some meeting. Pranav told me you would be joining them separately since you were coming from home."

Revathi was shocked. She remembered Pranav returning home really late and telling her that he had been working with Sonal. But that he should have gone out for dinner with Sonal and that too hidden it from her was unprecedented. She was hurt. From her confused reaction, Prabhakar too could make out that all wasn't really well between Revathi and her husband.

That evening Revathi got her salary cheque. On her way home, she decided to do some shopping and landed up at the Shoppers' Stop near the Andheri Station. Revathi was picking up a shirt for Pranav, when she saw Pranav standing just a few meters away. At first she thought it must have been an illusion. But it was not. Pranav and Sonal were actually shopping together. They were looking for the right pair of sunglasses. Revathi moved in their direction. Sonal saw her coming and alerted Pranav. Pranav looked stumped.

"Rr..re..revathi..oh, we were just returning from a meeting at Star's Sakinaka office. Since its Sonal's friend's birthday, I was helping her buy a gift."

Revathi did not speak a word. She just gave a long disappointed stare before walking off. And that stare said it all. Pranav left everything and followed her.

On their way home, they had an agitated discussion in the car. Revathi, in a no-nonsense, unambiguous and firm way, spelt out what she felt about the situation.

"Look, Pranav, we have always been very democratic towards each other's decisions. You haven't interfered with mine and I haven't with yours. I trust you completely but I'm sure, when we live in society, apart from being accountable to each other, we ought to be careful about the way we behave in front of people. Your closeness with Sonal is sending wrong perceptions. It's about time you realize it. "

Pranav agreed with her. In fact, he promised to be careful and keep a distance.

However, Revathi had been expecting more. Pranav had recently been offered the post of Creative Director and Partner by a leading advertising agency that had floated its own production house. Revathi had been insisting he take that up. Pranav, on the other hand, was just not prepared to work under somebody yet again.

When Revathi gave a piece of her mind to Pranav today, she somehow hoped he would understand her discomfiture with Sonal. For, in Revathi's assessment, Pranav's decision to get into production had a lot to do with what Sonal really wanted, rather than Pranav himself passionately wanting to pursue it. Revathi had been realizing that Pranav was not cut out to meet the rather whimsical demands of broadcasters. Shooting ad films suited him better. But then she could only suggest. In the past, her suggestions had their impact, but now, things seemed to be different. There were clear differences in the way Pranav and Revathi perceived situations.

The happy family was beginning to come to terms with having to cope with some not-too-happy times as well.

6

Get Set Gay – Part 1

Anil returned home by about eight in the evening and sauntered his way into the living room. Rupali was not yet in; she was off to Pune for some official work and was expected to return only late in the night. Anil came across an issue of FEMINA, lying on the center table. Rupali was a keen reader of the magazine. The cover had a model torn in dilemma and the supporting caption read, "Are you in love with two men?" This instantly whetted Anil's curiosity to read the whole story.

There was universal talk that marriages were not holding. India was passing through a phase of massive changes in all spheres and there was no way it could have possibly remained immune to western societal influences. The urban Indian populace had begun to show the same symptoms of dysfunction that was once the domain of the prurient west.

With time, Anil too had shed some of the orthodoxy that marked his growing years. For instance, all his life, he had never once seen his mother question his father's decisions. And he was brought up, not in the interiors of rural Maharashtra, but right in

Mumbai's backyard, Thane. The only rights given to his Aayee concerned the maintenance of the house – cooking, upkeep, servants, *pooja-paatth* and so on. And she didn't in the least mind mastering them rather than explore territories where she was not welcome.

However, two decades is a long period to change a person's mental set up. And the change was evident in Anil. His equation vis-à-vis his wife at times appeared just opposite of what it had been between his father and mother. Rupali, undoubtedly seemed to be the dominant partner in most matters and not without reasons.

Anil and Rupali had first met nearly four years ago at an export house. Anil, then a newly qualified CA, had come to the company to audit its accounts. Rupali, a cost accountant worked with the company. Rupali was seeing a guy called Manish from her college days. Hence Anil was forced to nip in the bud the instant attraction he felt for her.

Six months later, he came to the export house again. To his surprise, Rupali was no longer what she used to be. She had mellowed down considerably. The infectious camaraderie that Anil had associated with her seemed like a thing of the past. He learnt that Rupali and Manish had broken off. Manish, a software engineer had subsequently decided to migrate to the US. It was a coincidence that the phase when Rupali was at her worst emotional state, she was spending nearly half the day interacting with Anil professionally. Anil sensed her hurt and made her open up to him. They became friends and started confiding in each other.

Two years later, Anil and Rupali were contemplating marriage. It was more Anil's need because Rupali had realized that she was yet to get Manish out of her psyche completely. Anil was aware of it and almost consciously ignored the problem; such was his emotional dependence on Rupali by then. Rupali often wondered if she deserved the kind of importance that Anil gave her. As far as Anil was concerned, perhaps there was some form of desperation in his fondness. He realized that the matches that his parents were getting for him failed to meet his basic expectations. Matters, eventually, reached a point where if Anil had not furnished Rupali before his parents on the day he did, his parents would have fixed up his marriage with another girl— a typical orthodox marathi mulgi, Snigdha Pawar.

Besides, Rupali did impress his parents in parts, if not entirely. She was a Maharashtrian and a Deshasta Brahmin at that. They were only 96 Kuli Marathas. What they were a little apprehensive about was that Rupali had a more cosmopolitan outlook. Rupali had lived in different cities, thanks to her father's transferable Central Government job; hence they were not too sure if she would be able to uphold the conservative Marathi traditions their son had been brought up in.

Anil marketed Rupali to his parents as best he could and succeeded. Rupali and he soon got married. However, soon after marriage, the problem that Anil had conveniently ignored thus far, started to eat into him. He realized that though Rupali and he had become man and wife, the path to becoming soul mates still looked increasingly fraught with near improbabilities. Rupali was perhaps still to get out of the mode of being pampered and baby sat, like it happened in the first few months of their relationship when Rupali had been nursing her heartbreak. Besides, Anil had always been so protective of her that she had, without realizing it, come to be like an obstinate child who would have her way all the time. So when Anil at times wanted to make love and she didn't feel up to it, she would not hesitate to tell him so and go off to sleep. At the same time, when she was in the mood, she made sure that Anil fulfilled all her fantasies just the way she wanted it. There were other occasions when Anil would want to go out for a movie but she would be consumed with a self-imposed deadline to complete a book. And the strange thing was that she behaved with a lot of innocence, as though, she did not know that Anil was quietly suffering.

However, in the last few weeks, tension had aggravated between the two. Anil felt that it was about time they went for a child whereas Rupali was not ready for it yet. Rather, she sought to immerse herself in work and would even return home late, in order to avoid discussions on the subject. And this had been leading up to a silent estrangement between the two.

It was around a quarter past nine now. Anil had read the FEMINA story. It was basically a compilation of real life cases that were not entirely unknown to him. Your first love is the truest love that can never be substituted, he conjectured. The problem in his case was that while Rupali was his first love, he wasn't hers. It was a problem he had felt they would get over with in time but it was not to be. There was no way he could look like or be Manish, he lamented. In his state of rumination, he switched on the TV and did some aimless channel surfing. On Zee he came across this serial called Astitva that showed the relationship of an ex-husband and ex-wife. The ex-husband, invariably seemed besotted by his ex-wife while his present wife yearned "to own" him completely. This gave him food for imagination. What if Manish were to suddenly resurface? Would his wife be besotted by Manish just like the ex-husband seemed to be on his ex-wife in the serial?

Anil kept mulling for a definite answer that eluded him. At about ten in the night, Rupali called and informed him that she would be held up in Pune that night as the work was yet incomplete. Another half an hour later, Anil was beginning to have his meal, when he got a call. He was a little surprised to see the number flashing on the screen. It was Akash, the ex-Advertising Manager of the website.

"Hi Akash."

"Hi, I was just passing by your locality. I remembered you and thought that I should find out how you have been."

"Oh! Good! Man... how about you?"

"Great! You would be knowing, I'm currently working with a special interest magazine"

The conversation had to end abruptly as Akash was getting another call and promised to call Anil back. Anil waited for about fifteen minutes but Akash did not call back. Anil did not want to make the call himself for certain apprehensions. However another five minutes later, he had a change of mind. Coping with depressing forlornness, he decided that having Akash for company would at least make him feel better for sometime. Besides, Akash couldn't force him into anything. He dialed Akash's number to call him over.

Half an hour later Akash and Anil were chatting over coffee. Akash always had this thing of being able to make people talk their hearts out to him. Sensing that Anil was upset, he made Anil speak out the problem. And Anil did so, even though he realized whom he was speaking to.

"Hmmm! So that's your problem. Well, my friend, marriages are always complex. That's why I've steered clear of them."

Anil knew what the true reason was but in the state that he was in, he simply didn't feel like contradicting anything that Akash said.

"But it must be difficult for a married man to live in this

unfulfilled manner," Akash started manipulating the conversation.

Anil nodded faintly, not knowing where the empathy would lead.

"But tell me, what do you see the solution to be? I mean you've tried to make things work but they haven't. One way, is to keep fighting; the other is to find love elsewhere. Okay, be honest with me, haven't you ever been tempted to seek love in another female...let's say in a one night stand? "

"No. Never!" Anil put up a brave and principled front. "I will never cheat on my wife."

"That's good. You're a strong person. But what if in this situation, a gay made a pass at you?"

Anil knew that what he feared the most had happened. With that last sentence of Akash, he knew he had indeed been propositioned.

Akash and Anil went back a couple of years. When Anil joined themaltchmaker.com, Akash happened to be the Advertising Manager of the website. He belonged to a rich family and was flamboyant by nature. He stayed in a posh locality of Santacruz and traveled in a chauffeur driven Maruti Esteem. He was said to have a phobia of driving. He had a full time servant in his house- a young Kashmiri boy, who many believed was there for an ulterior purpose.

Akash was a gay or that's what everybody believed. Tall and with a prominent French beard, he was a glib talker who could make friends with anybody he wanted. Most of his friends were tall and able-bodied men— the model kinds to be more precise.

Akash was in this habit of calling friends over for dinner and making them stay over at his place on the pretext of watching a movie and then chatting. He had this ability to arouse the listener sexually by discussing sex in its barest graphic forms. He would also suitably supplement his talk with a rare collection of pornographic pictures and MMSs he had stored on his cell phone. The moment the listener experienced a hard on, Akash knew his ploy had worked. He would caress the hard on and take the act to its logical end. Hearsay had it that he was an incredibly good sucker.

Akash had made some concerted overtures to Anil just prior to Anil's marriage. Anil, at that point, did not know how to handle these overtures and had felt really scared.

Anil's most predominant memory of an instance involving a gay was the image of an effeminate vegetable vendor being beaten up publicly for having taken a young boy aside and felt his organs. This incident, which he must have witnessed in his early teens, had formed the unforgettable image with which he painted all gays. At one point, Anil had even complained to Vishal about Akash's overtures, as Vishal and Akash were good friends.

"But what's your problem? All you need to do is stand in one position and let him do what he has to. Believe me, you are going to thoroughly enjoy it," Vishal had advised.

Anil was stunned by this permissiveness towards 'perversion'. Thereafter, he took his own course and shunned Akash, barely even speaking to him, except officially, till Akash quit the job about six months back. On the day that Akash was given his farewell, he had hugged Anil hard and then smiled like a senior who was through with ragging his junior. And surprisingly when they spoke as friends that day, Anil was impressed with Akash's sensitivity, traces of which he had seen in his early days in the company, before Akash became more desperate. Anil realized that he had perhaps been too judgmental and even empathized with Akash.

Today, when Akash called him an hour ago, Anil had felt two disparate forces active in his mind. One, of course, warned him against the sleazy ways that Akash was known for, the other made him want to talk to him on a one-to-one level and share his forlornness over a sensitive interaction. Of course, the latter had prevailed over the former. But was he already regretting?

"Hey, you still haven't answered me? What would you do if a gay…?

Anil again digressed and flipped through the TV channels.

"Nowadays, music videos are so bloody provocative."

Anil was, on the surface, pretending to be occupied with TV but in his mind, he was actually meticulously assessing the extent to which Akash could go if Anil gave in. Akash, for his part, was consciously avoiding a caller on his cell, which he had already put on the silent mode.

Anil remembered another incident, this time from his college going days.

Anil used to go for Accounts tuition to a professor, Mr. Khan. Khan was a fair skinned gentleman with thin beard painted maroon. He must have been in his mid forties and was extremely soft spoken and well behaved, almost avuncular. He would constantly pull up Anil and give him tips on body language. Anil too found his concern almost fatherly. One day, Mr. Khan called Anil over separately. Anil did not read much into it as the tutor had in the past been known to take 'exclusive sessions' with his students.

Once there, Mr. Khan surprised Anil with his observation of his students' body languages. He had observed every gesture and every bodily movement to the minutest detail. What did not amuse Anil, though, was the area of the body he dwelt upon.

"Look, getting a decent percentage and clearing your papers is one thing. But once you enter the corporate world, it's your personality that matters." Mr. Khan preached and Anil found it genuine because even some of his peers were saying similar things.

"And your personality has a lot to do with the glow on your face. The glow on your face depends on your confidence and you feel confident when people look at you. But why will people look at you?"

Anil had no answer. He was conscious of his unimpressive looks.

"Have you ever seen the 'chalu' girls of today? Have you noticed that their undergarments leave a clear shape on their trousers?"

Anil was by now wondering why Mr. Khan was telling him about these chalu girls.

"Yes. I have."

"Look that's how a girl attracts men. Given an option, let me tell you that any employer would like to employ those girls whose undergarment's shape he can see for himself. It whets his fantasies."

"Yes, but why are you telling me all this?"

"Because, unlike these girls, you guys are fools. You don't know how to attract people towards you. Believe me, it's all a game of body language."

Anil still had no clue about where the conversation was heading till Mr. Khan convinced him to take a few exercises.

"Okay, come on take your pants down," instructed Khan, out of the blue.

"What?" Anil thought Khan was joking.

"Come on, don't question me. Do as I say."

Anil did so, the suddenness of things not allowing him an opportunity to think. Khan affectionately fondled Anil's organs till they were erect. And then he had Anil see his face in the mirror. There was a juvenile youthful smile, laced in good measure with notoriety.

"Look, that's the smile you got to have on your face when you meet people. And it can happen only when you feel "sexually confident".

After having a thorough, no-holds-barred feel of Anil's organs for some ten minutes, Khan advised him on how exactly to put on the under wear for a 'protruding' effect. Anil actually thanked him for the counsel, still obfuscated about the entire episode. Mr. Khan then asked him to come for an advanced second session next week. He instructed Anil to wash the organ properly before coming. But Anil never went; neither for the session on body language, nor for the Accounts tuition.

"So what are you thinking, my friend?" Akash probed yet again.

Anil somehow felt that all gays were alike and that Akash would actually complete the advanced session that Mr. Khan had talked about. Anil didn't know what went on in his mind but he actually took his trouser off and exposed what Akash craved for.

Akash for once was stunned by the ease with which it had ultimately happened. However, he also seemed disturbed by the incessant calling on his cell.

"Bloody bastards! Some guys just get on to your nerves." He switched off his cell. "Sorry.." He turned to concentrate on Anil. Within seconds, his face glowed with the same hunger that Anil had seen on Mr. Khan's face

"But remember. I'll only allow you to give me a blowjob, nothing beyond that. I know you are a good sucker," Anil forewarned.

Akash agreed, realizing it was not bad to start with. Perhaps he was not expecting even that. The act started in much the same manner as Khan had done, with Akash caressing and playing with Anil's dick. To Akash's surprise, it was reasonably long and well toned for someone Anil's height and built.

Anil was nervous initially, given Akash's wild reputation. He feared Akash would cross the limits. He was dead scared of a dick penetrating him. But realizing the stakes, Akash handled him with great care, almost like a doctor.

However, once Anil felt more reassured, Akash progressed to wilder activities. He sucked, chewed, licked and did everything he could to make Anil feel like God. And Anil did, for a change, feel like the dominant partner. In one particular posture, Akash looked like a slave, his neck trapped between Anil's legs, as Anil lay on bed. To exploit the act of being master further, Anil pulled Akash by his hair and positioned him the way he wanted. Anil wondered if there was something really nutritional about his organ for Akash just sucked it on and on. Akash's dedication aroused Anil's curiosity.

"Hey, isn't there a risk in what you do?" he asked.

Akash just smiled. "Don't worry, dude. That's the reason we go for timid one-woman men like you. You think I'll ever do this to Vishal? Nahhhhh!"

Anil was impressed. These gays planned their prowl so well, he thought.

Akash's finesse, then, had him give periodic soft pecks to Anil in certain high response zones like the "G" spot, as also in the small stretch of skin between his balls and the ass-hole. These added bonuses filled up Anil with unmatched ecstasy.

The act went on for almost an hour. By the time it ended, Anil was magically relieved of all his worries. He felt gratified and wished Rupali could do the job half as good.

Akash, for his part, respected the limits he had been given. He chose not to go beyond.

"I swear I've never had such fun with my wife," gushed Anil, oblivious that his remark would raise his partner's expectations.

"But next time, if you come, it will be on my terms," cautioned Akash.

Anil realized that Akash had presumed that he was on for a second time. Anil didn't feel like confronting him on this. Not right away, at least.

That night, Akash left soon after. The thrill of the experience, however, kept Anil awake the whole night. He must have slept only by morning. At 8, the doorbell rang. He wondered who it could be. Rupali couldn't come from Pune that early, or maybe she started off at 4, he thought. Anil looked through the peeping glass.

There was Rupali and there were three policemen, one of whom looked like being of Inspector rank. It was quite a bizarre combination actually. What added to the absurdity was Rupali arguing with them that her husband was innocent. Anil had no idea what was happening. He opened the door.

"Mr. Anil Sapre?" the inspector charged.

Anil nodded. "What's the matter?"

"Your friend Akash was murdered late last night. His chauffeur has told us that he was with you till about 2-30am. We suspect your hand in it. You are under arrest."

---

* *Play safe. Use Condoms.*

7

Ah! The Plot Thickens

"Wow! This is really amazing!" beamed Revathi, when Pranav showed her a printout of the story featuring the couple. "Apart from being so positive, it is indeed very well written. What do you feel?"

"Yeah, and the best thing about it is that it shows us as a happy couple," teased Pranav.

The story was part of a regular feature on thematchmaker.com that carried a write up on one happily married couple every fortnight. It was Mayank's brainchild. He thought it would provide fodder for prolonged communication with Revathi; hence he employed Vishal to do the story. Vishal, the Samaritan, did not see any significant reason why the couple could not be featured as long as it served Mayank a purpose. Besides, a reputed ad-filmmaker and the brand manager of a reputed "Marriage Store" did make an illustrious media couple anyway.

"I think I must call up Mayank and thank him for this," said Revathi.

"This guy, Mayank is interesting it seems. And I suppose, he gets along well with you."

"Well, he's mature beyond his years. When you talk to him, you won't feel you're talking to someone much younger to you."

"Is he married?"

"No. In fact he shifted to the city only six months back."

"Hmmm. Interesting. Then, why don't you call him home some time. I would like to meet this young friend of yours."

Revathi was a little surprised by the keenness shown by Pranav. After all, in the last few months his professional problems had led him to almost alienate himself socially.

"Do you really want to meet him?" she asked, nearly doubting him.

"Yeah… Why not? Staying alone in the city makes people look for company. Call him over for dinner. He'll feel good and that would be a nice way to thank him for this article."

"That's really nice of you, Pranav. When should we call him?"

"Well… How's Friday? I have this presentation at Star on Friday, after which we could have him over for dinner."

Revathi called up Mayank the next morning, just as he was about to leave for office. Her dinner invitation had Mayank's heart skip a beat. Throughout his journey to the office that day, he kept wondering what Revathi would look like when he went to her place for dinner. From his first two meetings, he knew that she was quite comfortable in salwar kameez; maybe this time, she would sport a funkier color, say pink. In another instant, he imagined how she would have done up her house; after all, she looked like a person with refined tastes.

However, a day before the proposed dinner, Pranav and Revathi had a major spat. The reason was Sonal. Sonal had used Ria's computer the whole day in preparing for the Star presentation. In the process Ria could not complete an important school assignment. What irked Revathi later was the fact that Pranav knew about Ria's assignment, yet did not stop Sonal.

"Pranav, there's a limit. I understand Sonal and you are working together but that doesn't mean she should use our house for everything."

"What do you mean by everything? Don't you know how important this presentation is for us?"

"I know that, but why can't she prepare it on her own computer?"

"Look that's not how a creative industry works. We need to discuss so many ideas every moment and for that she needs to be here."

"Pranav, look, I shouldn't be saying this but I get this impression that she is just looking for excuses to be here."

"Really? Stop it, Revathi. Sometimes you talk such crap."

Pranav had turned to go out of the room when Revathi retorted.

"I talk crap? It's become useless to even talk to you, Pranav, you're going senile."

"Oh, shut up now."

It had been one of those intense skirmishes that previously erupted once in a blue moon; now it would be once in a few weeks. As a result of it, Revathi was deprived of the ritual that Pranav employed to wake her up the next morning. Revathi did wish Pranav luck at the breakfast table but Pranav remained rather cold. Later, just before the presentation, Revathi called him up from office and made up with a conjured apology, just to make sure that Pranav was in a good mood at the time of presentation.

At about eight in the evening, Mayank arrived. Having worked his way up the sixteen floors, he came across this name board at the door that read 'The Padgaonkars'. The maid opened it and led him into the living room. He was quite impressed by the way it had been done up. The walls were coated tastefully with dark teakwood. The living room was endowed with all the accoutrements that one is normally wont to expect in an upper middle class living room. It had a lavish cream-colored sofa set, a huge glass cupboard that showcased a rich collection of books, a couple of bean bags and a home theatre. One book that prominently stood out of the collection was Vikram Chandra's *Love and Longing in Bombay*. Mayank wondered if Revathi really liked it and almost instantly thought that there could be either love or longing in a married woman's life. If there were both, it reeked of a fluid situation in one's marriage. He also noticed a framed photograph of Revathi and her husband, from their younger days on a holiday abroad.

About a third of the area of the living room was elevated. It had a small round table with four chairs, perhaps for dinner or conferencing, or both. The round table almost bordered the outer glass wall that gave a bird's eye view of the suburbs.

Mayank sat for about ten minutes before Revathi arrived. This time around she was not in salwar kameej. Instead, she was in a red round neck T-shirt and jeans. Her attire made her look at least half a decade younger and that much more unencumbered. Her hair was neatly done up. Mayank wondered why long hair often made a female look sexier.

"Hi, so how have you been?"

"Oh, Good! How about you?"

"Okay." She remarked in a mellowed voice that sounded almost strained. "Actually a woman in the dual responsibilities of home-maker and a professional is seldom very good."

"Have I come at a wrong time? You sound a bit hassled."

"Oh, no, no. It's nothing like that. It's the usual set of problems. My maid wants to go on leave for a week beginning the day after. My chauffeur bunks as and when he wants and then gives the lame excuse of rains. It all becomes very irksome when there is so much pressure on the professional front."

Mayank heard it out patiently. He could sense somehow that there was more to her anguish than just her maid and her chauffeur. As far as maid and the chauffeur were concerned, he realized he couldn't possibly do much. He wouldn't have minded being her chauffeur, though.

"Your husband isn't home?" Mayank queried in curiosity.

"He must be in any moment now. He had an important presentation that got delayed."

Revathi informed him about her husband trying to foray into software production.

"So is he not doing ad-films at all now?"

"No, it's not that actually. Well, I guess when a creative person reaches his peak too early, all his life he has to cope with the pressure of living up to the standards that he has set for himself. It becomes really difficult to do ordinary work and live like an ordinary professional. Pranav doesn't want to do ad-films unless they are really exciting. At the same time, the really exciting offers are going to the younger makers -- the new kids on the block."

"Hmmmm…"

"So now he wants to sit back for a while and just organize talent. He wants to produce TV software."

"That's interesting. Aren't you involved with it?"

"Well, no. It's a very unpredictable profession. At least I am earning well and that enables us to keep up our standards."

Revathi did not realize that in a very unknowing way, she had candidly divulged that her house was running on her income.

"But tell me Ma'am, are you a Maharashtrian? You don't look or sound like one."

Revathi laughed.

"Well, no, we're from U.P., Kankakubya Brahmins, if you've heard of them."

"Okay, so got married to a Maharashtrian?"

"Yes."

Revathi narrated briefly her fairy tale that led her to become a Padgaonkar. Mayank, the keen observer that he was, sensed that the nostalgia evoked in her when she spoke about those days had an almost melancholic tinge rather than a happy one. 'Was she devoid of the same happiness in her relationship now?' he wondered.

"Interesting. Really interesting. It's the sort of stories that Hindi films are made of," Mayank chipped in quickly, trying to conceal the uncertain meandering of thoughts in his mind.

"Or perhaps, Pranav was so influenced by some Hindi movie that he was determined to fall in love in much the same manner," Revathi teased her husband, safely so, in his absence.

By now, the strain that could be sensed in her voice a little while ago had been significantly done away with. And this Mayank thought, was an indicator that she had begun to enjoy making conversation to him.

At that point, a little kid came and stood respectfully at the door, waiting for Revathi to take notice. And when Revathi did spot her, the kid asked cutely," Mom, can I come in?"

"Yes, beta."

"Mom, I've completed my homework and don't have anything else to do."

Revathi introduced Mayank to her daughter, Ria. She then took Ria in her lap, smothered her with kisses and then asked Ria to sit on the sofa beside her. Ria did so obediently. Mayank made out that Ria was an extremely well groomed kid.

"How old is she, Ma'am?"

"I think you should stop calling me ma'am, now. You may call me by my name."

"Okay, ma'am… sorry… I mean, Revathi." Mayank sounded formal and even a trifle awkward accepting the concession, though he had been expecting it.

'She is eight."

At that point, Revathi got a call on her cell. "Hello, ya Shruti? Where are you now? We'd been trying to call…" Revathi moved out of the room, speaking on her cell. The manner in which she took the call showed urgency and concern, and Mayank wondered if all was well. Perhaps it was something personal that she did not want to share, he thought. He couldn't make out what it was but at least was glad that the caller was a female.

This gave Mayank an opportunity to mingle with the little Ria and they got along quite well.

Revathi returned after about ten minutes. She looked disturbed again. Mayank just tried to figure out if she wanted to share the cause. And Revathi told him that it had to do with her sister, Shruti, who was in the US.

"Shruti is in love with a Pakistani guy settled in the US. My Mom is dead opposed to the relationship."

Mayank gave a concerned empathetic look, as there was little he could do beyond that.

"What do your parents do?"

"Well, my Dad is no more. My Mom is a senior journalist.

Her name is Rohini Tiwari."

"What? She's your Mom?"

Rohini had been in news recently for being nominated to the Rajya Sabha.

Mayank realized that Revathi had quite an assortment of illustrious people around her. Yet her simplicity would not give a clue of it when someone met her for the first time.

Revathi remained preoccupied, though, perhaps in her sister's problem.

"My sister is about your age. At one point, we were very close but I don't know what happened then. Perhaps the Indian society underwent such a sudden change in the nineties that I started feeling as though there was a generation gap between my sister and me. She suddenly started hating my involvement with her life and did just the opposite of what I told her."

Mayank could sense an almost maternal instinct in Revathi when she spoke these last few sentences. He surmised that elder siblings mostly did tend to behave like parents and 'control' the lives of the younger siblings. It often did not go well with the younger siblings. He had had a similar problem with his younger brother.

"Dunno where Pranav is held up. He should have been here by now."

Revathi realized that the conversation was tending to be gloomy and tried seeping in some positivism.

"Okay, tell me about your marriage plans?"

"Well, I'm already engaged."

"Wow. Congratulations! So marriage must be round the corner."

"I don't know." Mayank sounded staid.

Revathi wondered the cause of such nonchalance in Mayank.

"You must be happy about it," she probed mildly.

"Well, I don't know if I'm marrying the right girl."

Mayank explained the situation in which he got engaged to Rewa, the perceptions he always entertained about his potential wife and his near skepticism towards the institution of arranged marriage.

"You know, I feel you're being cynical. The problem with intelligent men is that they think too much. And sometimes, the more you think the more problems you imagine for yourself, problems which may actually not exist at all." Revathi almost sounded like a psychologist.

Revathi's words struck Mayank like lightning. Shweta had once said exactly the same thing to him. Of course it was in a different context. At that point the confusion pertained to Mayank's career options. For a while, Mayank looked completely lost.

"What happened? Why are you suddenly looking so lost?" Revathi asked, sensing a sudden disturbance in Mayank.

Mayank ended up telling her about how her words had reminded her about Shweta, the girl he had loved.

As the conversation went further, a clear picture began to emerge, albeit subconsciously, in Mayank's mind about the kind of woman that he was exactly looking for. He was looking for someone like Revathi. Yes, it was indeed an inescapable truth that was beginning to dawn upon him.

"In fact, my fiancé, Rewa will be coming here in the first week of August. She has a job interview. I think it will be great if you can meet her. Let's see what you feel about her."

Revathi wasn't sure about Mayank's motive in asking her to meet Rewa. Neither was she that close to him, not yet. Nonetheless, she found it an innocuous exercise, hence agreed.

"Okay, show me your palm," she said, apparently to engage in some absorbing talk. At the back of her mind there was worry concerning Pranav's presentation and why he hadn't returned yet.

"Do you know palmistry?" asked Mayank with surprise.

"A bit of it."

Mayank showed her his palm.

"What's your star sign, Ma'am?"

"I'm a Leon. In fact, my birthday is round the corner. It's on the 7th August. What about you?"

"Virgo. 11 September."

After a careful examination of Mayank's palm, she bore a somewhat worried expression.

"Hey, wait! It looks like there are two marriages for you."

"What?"

"No, no, hang on."

Revathi concentrated harder and then finally concluded: "No, the upper one is actually not fructifying into marriage. It'll only be an affair or a strong emotional involvement. But in the process it will delay your marriage." In an afterthought, she added, "By the way, there are obstacles even on the second line, which means your marriage is not going to be an easy process."

Mayank couldn't but agree with the stark truth in what Revathi had said. He recalled an incident that had happened several years ago. As a first year graduation student in Delhi's Hindu College, he had come across an MA Sanskrit student who would make forecasts based on palmistry with amazing precision. This enlightened student had said more or less the same words. The first line, he gathered later was Shweta. He didn't know yet who would be the second line.

Mayank wondered if in his case the time had come for palmistry to go real.

"Show me your palm," said Mayank.

Revathi wondered if he too knew a thing or two about palmistry, but since she was not the sort who asked too many questions, she obliged. From whatever Mayank had known of palmistry over the years, he knew that trouble was brewing in her marriage. He wouldn't say so, however, for fear that what he had known of palmistry could be wrong.

He held her hand and observed it intently. In normal situations, it may have looked a bit awkward. But in the absorbing conversation that had been the prelude to it, it didn't look all that odd. At least that is probably why Revathi did not protest, he thought. Perhaps she too was anticipating some soothing predictions.

Right at this point, Pranav entered. Sonal was in tow. Pranav looked hassled. It was understandable, perhaps, knowing where he was coming from. And of course, the sight of this young guy ogling at his wife's hands did not make Pranav any happier.

Revathi introduced Mayank to Pranav. After a formal exchange of greetings, Pranav quickly excused himself and went inside. Sensing that all was not well, Revathi followed him. This left Mayank and Sonal in the room.

"What happened, Pranav? How did it go?" Revathi asked out of concern.

"What happens at these meetings? No matter what these channels claim, fact is that they are just petrified to come out of the rut of saas-bahu sagas. They just can't accept anything that's different. Damn it." Pranav banged his foot in disarray.

"Relax! Pranav. We'll think of something. Just forget it for the time being. We'll talk about it later."

"Yeah, you carry on. I'll take a shower before I join you guys."

"Is Sonal also joining us for dinner?"

"No, I just got to give her a floppy before she leaves."

"It's okay if she joins."

"No need."

About half an hour later, Pranav, Revathi and Mayank were having dinner. Pranav carried his frustration over to the dinner table.

"I tell you, these channel people can be such pain to deal with it. The biggest problem with these morons is that they know what they don't want but don't have the slightest clue about what they want."

Abject frustration was only too obvious in Pranav's tenor. And while it embarrassed Revathi, Pranav himself did not quite realize it. Mayank found it a little strange, given that it contradicted the image he had of Pranav. Just over five years ago when Mayank was studying MBA, he had read an interview of Pranav in A&M and was in awe of the man.

Revathi skillfully maneuvered a change of topic. However, Pranav's crotchety disposition was difficult to be entirely wished away. Pranav seemed somewhat idiosyncratic as well. For instance, Mayank was a little surprised to find that Pranav did not carry a cell phone.

"One mustn't depend on these gadgets. Besides they are a health hazard. I mean it's a proven fact that they damage your brain cells."

Mayank found it somewhat difficult to interact freely with Pranav. There was some snootiness in him, which Mayank thought must have been carried forward from his successful days. Perhaps,

Pranav had raised himself to a pedestal from where he found it difficult to come down. Whatever, it was, he was a huge contrast from Revathi's uncomplicated self. Mayank, however, tried to be at his respectful best for the next one hour, till the evening was through.

⌒

A week later, it was Revathi's birthday. As expected, the ritual of waking her up went on a little longer than usual. It would have gone on possibly the whole day, had Revathi been more co-operative.

About half an hour later, Pranav walked into the living room. He was pleased to find Revathi, still in her nightgown, reading a birthday card. On her lap was a small basket of red roses. Revathi finished reading the card and smiled. Pranav smiled back.

"So how do you find the roses?"

"Oh, lovely."

"It's strange... I'd ordered for a more wholesome bouquet, but looks like the florist knew your taste better... he sent only roses. That too special red ones."

"Well...these roses have actually been sent by Mayank."

Pranav had a thoroughly obfuscated expression when he heard this. Before he could react, however, the doorbell rang. Pranav opened it to find the florist's guy standing with the bouquet. He apologized to Pranav for being late.

Pranav gifted the bouquet to Revathi. He realized that they couldn't evoke the same sparkle in her eyes that the roses did. He recalled her first birthday post marriage, when he had had the whole living room decorated with roses. Pranav wondered what could have made him forget her liking for the red roses now. That was something she had made known to him even in their courtship days. He was equally startled wondering how Mayank knew about it or was it sheer coincidence.

Revathi's birthday brought in good luck for Pranav. He got a letter from Sony asking him to shoot the 'pilot' for a concept that Pranav had given them three months ago. Pranav was clearly elated.

That evening, the family went out for dinner. Thrice during the course of the dinner, Revathi was disturbed by calls on her cell phone. It was from a nervous Mayank. Mayank seemed to be diligently working out the logistics of making Revathi meet Rewa, who was coming down from Delhi the day after. Even though the calls were long and hindered the conversation between the family members, Revathi quite took it in her stride. Pranav got bugged though.

That night, as they lay in bed, Revathi was unusually pepped up. She wanted to engage Pranav in conversation. However, Pranav seemed preoccupied. She thought he'd be thinking about the pilot that he had to shoot. When she probed the matter, her husband gave her quite a shock.

"I somehow don't quite like this friend of yours, Mayank."

8

Painful Ecstasy – Part 1

Vishal walked into the office terribly upset. His frazzled expression couldn't hide that something really absurd must have happened at home. Vishal ignored Tina's greeting and proceeded straight into his cubicle. There he indulged himself in a game of cards on his computer.

That Gargi and he were poles apart was a well known fact... However, in the past couple of weeks, things had only got worse between the two. One of the main causes for this tension was the couple's inability to conceive. Gargi had realized that beyond a point she could not expect her husband to change or to come around to being the way she wanted him to be. Gargi, therefore, had even stopped asking Vishal where he had been, even when he landed up at midnight. Divorce was not an easy option for Gargi, either, as she knew her parents back in Meerut would never support her in it. Gargi's helpless situation had led her to having an atrociously bad temper.

On the advice of a friend, Gargi sought emotional succor in conceiving a baby, whose upbringing, she felt would consume much of her passion and time and enable her to ignore her husband for a few years. The idea of going in for a baby suited Vishal also. He too had been advised that Gargi's preoccupation with the baby might be the only way he could get his space. However when that too did not look like happening easily, the emptiness in their marriage and the disparities became all the more insurmountable. To deal with the near precarious situation, Gargi, one day, bought herself a Pomeranian. And guess what, even that caused a major fight between Vishal and Gargi because Vishal simply detested dogs.

Vishal played the game aimlessly for almost an hour when a phone call caused a disruption. The office looked relatively empty for a change. Anil was on a day's leave whereas Mayank was out for a meeting. The other employees carried out their daily chores in their respective workstations. Tina sensed that Vishal was in a foul mood. She too did not look to be in her elements for some unknown reason. Looking bored and upset, Tina walked up to Vishal and leaned against his cubicle. Vishal looked so anguished that he didn't quite realize that something unusual had happened. For, till today, Tina had been a sort of cock-teaser to him; always enticing him with her charm and sex appeal and then steering clear of him just when he got tempted to make a pass at her. Vishal was often confused with her; for never had a girl been so easy and yet so difficult to get, simultaneously. Then one day, Vishal was told that Tina was actually going steady with a guy from her college days and that they'd been together for a couple of years. Vishal gathered that although she sensed his attraction for her and was aware of his reputation, she was just being a loyal girlfriend, perhaps.

The Tina who he had known was a charmer, alright. With her infectious smile and a near perfect figure to boot, she could always capture a man's sexual fantasies; but when it came to making conversation, she faltered badly, not being able to speak English or Hindi correctly. Vishal felt that this was a problem endemic to most middle-of-the-road, lower middleclass Maharashtrians. Their ingrained aversion for the migrant Hindi-speaking populace hadn't left them with much respect to speak the language properly, and at the same time, the near parochial Marathi leanings had made sure that even when they spoke in English, it was affected with a strong vernacular accent.

Vishal loved native Mumbaiite girls, though, for they appeared enamored of the North Indian males more than some of the other girls that he had come across. And from the couple of experiences he had with them, what he liked most about them was a 'lets get on with it' attitude. They never asked too many questions and were more co-operative and sporting than their North Indian counterparts. Also, they knew before the act that it was a mutual need with no emotional hang overs later on.

With so many advantages, it was but obvious that Vishal had been thirsting to lay Tina.

And to Vishal's pleasant surprise, Tina looked in a more responsive mood today.

"What have you been up to? Not much work today?" she broke into a conversation.

"No...well, I have some work but just not in the mood...will do it later"

"Are you upset about something?"

Tina took an unusual interest in him, completely uncharacteristic of her so far. Her sullen face however was indicative of hurt and dejection, even though it made her appear more like a kid who had been kept away from gorging her favorite chocolates.

Vishal sensed that with this display of empathy, Tina perhaps wanted him to dig into her sorrow and give her a hearing. Not one to miss a cue like this, Vishal obliged. And what he heard surely made him skip a beat or two.

"Yes, we've broken off."

There was a moment's pause before Tina continued. "Well, love is the most beautiful and the most painful feeling on this earth. Girish and I were through with our beautiful moments...what remained was pain. And hence we thought it would be better to break off."

"But there surely must have been a valid reason?"

"Not a single reason... there were a few reasons that just got cluttered together and made it impossible to look further."

"Like?"

"Well, he could never trust me. Perhaps he had major inferiority complex that always kept him in fear that I was sleeping with other men."

"But why did he have such fears?"

"Girish is suspicious by nature. He never trusted his sister either."

"But tell me honestly, you do flirt with men, don't you?"

Tina took a pensive pause before answering.

"I do keep them in good humor; because, frankly, unless you keep a man 'interested' he will never be of any help to you."

Vishal was startled by this last remark that displayed Tina's insight of a man's mind. The girl, who he had always dismissed as dumb, did have some intelligent ways about her, he thought.

"What help do you expect from a man?' he probed her further, drenching himself into the topic.

"Look, a girl like me who doesn't have big degrees to back her, needs a charming persona to make people take notice of her. What qualifications does a receptionist need? And why should I have got the job over many other competent rivals? The only thing that goes in my favor is that I radiate a 'feel good' thing in men."

Vishal, by now was mesmerized by the planning that went into being what Tina was. Perhaps the two words 'feel good', once propounded by the erstwhile NDA government's poll managers had actually found an able executioner in this girl, he thought.

Vishal realized that within a span of a few minutes, Tina had opened up with him considerably. And this was enough to give him hope that given the state of mind she was in, she could very well be expected to go further. Vishal stuck to dwelling upon her break-up thereon and gave ample reason for Tina to believe that in him she had a shoulder she could lean on.

An hour later, the two were spotted having lunch together in a Lokhandwala restaurant. Vishal still found it difficult that Tina's break up had actually opened up the door for him big time. Besides, it was sheer coincidence that Tina's change of heart had to happen on the day that Vishal had the worst skirmish with his wife. Tina knew that even Vishal wasn't in the best of moods and took the opportunity to find out the reason.

"Well it's just that my wife and I are two very different people. She despises non-vegetarian food, I love it; she loves dogs, I hate them; she is an extremely reserved person, I freak out on parties. With such disparities, it is but obvious that we would end up fighting, which we do."

"Was it an arranged marriage?"

"No, it was an out-and-out love marriage."

"How come then, you couldn't see these disparities before?"

Vishal actually thought hard before he answered dispassionately.

"Actually everything has a proper time to it and that includes falling in love. In my case, well, I had been involved with a lot of women but somehow always shied away from the thought of marriage. I guess I had developed such a passion for screwing more and more women that I didn't realize age was quietly running away for me. So when a common friend introduced me to this simple, sweet and homely girl, I somehow got this feeling that it was time for me to put my escapades behind and settle down. After all, at 32, I wasn't getting any younger. Gargi used to be a customer service executive with the ICICI bank. We dated each other for a couple of months and then got married within the next two. It all seemed liked a fairytale till I realized that meeting somebody over a date was one thing, staying with the person as spouse another. The same qualities that endeared me to Gargi at one point, started seeming so alien when we actually started living as husband and wife."

Tina soaked in the narration intently.

Another hour went by without either realizing that they could become such instant confidants. After paying the bill, Vishal sat on for a little longer. He then carefully maneuvered the conversation to first thank Tina for the wonderful interaction they had; then he added, "I wish we could talk to each other like this the whole of today." As Vishal said that last bit, he ensured that the potent device of 'eye contact' was aptly put into play. Simultaneously, he held Tina's hand supportively. A glint appeared in his eyes, indicating what he was getting at.

Tina knew that she had been trapped and willingly so. She protested faintly, reasoning out that the office work would suffer.

Vishal countered it by saying that in any case they hadn't worked since morning; besides with Ramamurthy away, a couple of hours more won't make heavens fall. As he said that, he clasped her hand more firmly.

Another forty five minutes later, they occupied a third floor room in a three star hotel near the Malad Station. The seasoned player that Vishal was, he knew exactly how to go about the act. They were already in the middle of a booze session, having seeped in a glass each of Haywards 5000 beer. And when Tina showed the initial signs of feeling tipsy, Vishal knew it was time to 'start'.

It had been quite a while before Vishal was screwing someone so young and refreshingly lively. An idea suddenly struck him at that point as he remembered an incident from the past. He unbuttoned Tina's shirt. Tina stood nervously, a white bra covering her boobs, while the skirt below remained intact. Vishal felt her tits, clasping them between his two fingers, till Tina gave a sigh. Vishal then stripped himself down to his underwear- a red color VIP frenchie. Tina looked on curiously.

"Look, baby we're going to play a game. Each of us will have to completely strip the other and expose the other's hidden 'booty'. The one who does it first would get to exercise complete dominance over the sexual act that follows, while the other would be treated like a sex slave who would have to follow the partners' instructions."

This entire exercise reminded Vishal of an orgy that he had once indulged in with a girl in college. He thought, it was time once again, to relive all the madness that he had lost out on being with Gargi.

Tina showed reluctance initially but relented soon enough.

The game started. And the two virtually wrestled trying hard to strip the other.. The fight served the purpose of a sort of 'warm up' because once the bodies were heated up, the flow of hormones rose automatically to amazing levels; desires got propelled manifold. Vishal, of course, won it in the end and the 'booty' was all his to exploit.

Vishal couldn't believe his luck. From the way it was going, he knew that they were headed for a rare, mesmerizing experience. He chose to be more innovative in his improvisation.

Vishal began by blinding Tina with his handkerchief. He then used the ice that was meant to cool the liquor to rub it gently all over Tina's body. When Tina experienced this, her ecstasy knew no bounds. She flung her hands and legs in painful joy, invariably clasping Vishal's body with her legs. Vishal then raised her up so that both looked like the couple in one of Kamasutra's ads.

Vishal then made love to Tina – "fucked her royal" as he loved to call it; her eyes still covered. In her blindness, Tina sensed unprecedented satisfaction and Vishal could make out why her boyfriend had been so suspicious. Moreover, the blinding of Tina had left him with complete powers to manipulate her body; seeing her private parts react to the wild things he did brought rare orgasmic joy – something he had not experienced in any of his recent encounters.

As Tina gasped in ecstasy, Vishal finally took away his handkerchief and made her see the nakedness of all that she had joyfully experienced. He then followed it up with a passionate smooch on her lips…

The first spell had whetted Tina's appetite for more. Though she did not say it in as many words, her gratification revealed that her boyfriend had not been half as effective. The second spell of the act saw them bathing together in the bathtub and Vishal later followed it up with another round of boobs- fucking on the bed, this time with her eyes and mouth wide open.

At about five in the evening, they realized that a whole day had gone by and decided to return to office, one after the other at an interval of about twenty minutes.

Tina sat in the office way beyond her scheduled time, but remained as devoid of action as a woman in her last stages of pregnancy. The emotional turmoil of her break-up had by now given way to another emotional turmoil of a different kind. Coupled with it, was the physical stress of having borne an inexhaustible sex maniac.

Vishal, on the other hand, recovered more quickly and sat down to completing a story for which he had been given a deadline for that evening itself. The deadline held him in office till late in the evening and by the time Vishal reached home it was almost eleven.

Gargi, for some unknown reason, looked happy and graceful, just like she had looked when they first met. She did not ask him anything. Rather, she laid out the food quite dutifully. Vishal wondered why she was being so good. The huge altercation they had had in the morning, however, prevented either of them from broaching a conversation.

Later, when Vishal was through with his channel surfing and switched off the lights. Gargi finally broke the silence.

"Vishal, I have some good news to give you."

Vishal was too preoccupied to even remotely anticipate what it could be. At best, he had an inkling she may have decided to go in for divorce.

"Vishal, I'm carrying."

Much later that night, even when Gargi was fast asleep, slumber somehow eluded Vishal. He walked around the house abruptly, looked anguished and immersed himself in the smoke generated by umpteen cigarettes. Remorse had eclipsed the happiness that he and his wife had been longing for. For the first time, he felt ashamed of himself. Vishal's ecstasy was mired in pain.

---

* *Play safe. Use Condoms.*

9

Dependence

The D-day had come. Revathi was supposed to take an unusual test today. She had to decide for Mayank whether or not Rewa was the right girl for him. The thought of it made her feel important and at the same time nervous. It instilled an almost frightening sense of responsibility in her. After all, it was a task that involved her to pass an opinion that would have a bearing on someone else's life. Given that Revathi had always respected people's independent choices, she'd have surely been better off without being entrusted with such an onus.

Revathi wished though that her own sister, Shruti had considered her that important. And the thought took her to the past when on a vacation with her mother, the sisters had got down to discussing what sort of man would make worthy husband material for Shruti.

"Tall, dark, handsome, sensitive, sensible, ambitious, outgoing, intelligent yet abstract. Simply crazy," Shruti had replied with utmost surety.

Ironically it struck Revathi at this point that Mayank was quite like that. It would have been so nice in fact, if Shruti and Mayank could be paired, she thought. But then life is normally full of ironies that are known to take their own course— a course that by and large is different from what mortals wish; she philosophized. Revathi decided therefore not to waste her time on wishful thinking.

At a half past two, as per the plan Revathi met Mayank at Mahesh Lunch Home near Juhu Beach. They were supposed to have a quick lunch before meeting Rewa at the Mocha nearby. Mayank had thought of using the small lunch interaction with Revathi to acquaint her with the job she had to execute. Revathi, though, felt that Mayank was overdoing things.

"Look Mayank, Rewa has just come from Delhi in the morning. Instead of calling me here, you should have gone and personally got her to Mocha."

"Yeah, I should have. But then, now there is not much I can do. But she knows Mumbai pretty well… in fact her maternal uncle stays at Chembur."

"But this is not the way, Mayank."

Mayank did not have an answer. He knew he had been an inept host.

"Anyway, tell me about this special briefing for which you have called me here."

Mayank again did not quite know what to say.

"I've been feeling very nervous. Your presence makes me feel slightly better."

"What? That's it? Do you know that I've actually taken half a day off because you said you wanted to discuss something very, very important?"

Mayank was speechless. He instead called for the waiter.

"Look Mayank, it is not right for you to depend so much upon me. I'm not your girlfriend."

Mayank shot back almost out of the blue: "Then, why don't you get me the right girl?"

Revathi was stunned by this riposte. But having begun to know Mayank's traits, she chose not to react. After all, a casual, innocent sort of impertinence looked almost ingrained in his behavior. She knew by now that ignoring it was a better way to deal with it. By the time they were through with their lunch, it was almost a quarter past three. Prodded by Revathi, they made a beeline for Mocha.

At nearly 3:25, Mayank and Revathi rushed into Mocha. They were surprised to see Rewa already seated there.

"Hey, Rewa, I'm so sorry for the delay. I really didn't expect you would make it on time."

"No issues. But there wasn't much traffic on the way, so I couldn't possibly be late."

Mayank looked a little embarrassed even as Rewa wondered why this other lady had to be there.

"Okay, yes, at this time, it's a bit of an off hour. By the way, Rewa, this is my friend Revathi. And Revathi, this is my fiancée Rewa."

Revathi and Rewa exchanged greetings.

"So how was your interview?" Revathi initiated interaction.

"It was alright. It was for the post of an In house counselor in ICICI. They would let me know in a week."

"Psychology is a fascinating subject. It interests me a lot."

Rewa wondered what sort of friendship Mayank and Revathi shared. After all, for Revathi to be privy to a private meeting of theirs meant that the proximity must have been immense.

"Can we order for something?" asked Mayank.

"Yeah," both women nodded simultaneously.

"Here, Rewa, have a look at this menu," Revathi put forth the menu card in front of Rewa.

Before Rewa could even run through the entire card, Revathi intervened.

"I suggest you go for Sumatra Mandheling. You will find it almost exotic in this weather and ambience."

"Yeah, go for it. Revathi, mind you, is quite a connoisseur of the different coffee types available here."

Rewa opted for it, realizing she didn't have much of a choice. She kept wondering how many Mocha rendezvous Revathi and Mayank would have had together. Revathi looked older to Mayank for sure and looked married as well. At least she sported a chain around her neck, which Rewa couldn't make out if it was a *mangal sutra* or not. But you never know, open marriages perhaps may have ceased to be such a taboo thing in Mumbai; Rewa feared. Almost in an instant afterthought, she felt confident that Mayank would not be a part of such a thing. In another instant afterthought, she felt pretty confident that even Revathi would not be such a woman. She looked too graceful to indulge in anything that was not above board.

Within the next few minutes, coffee was laid out for them. However, when Rewa was shifting her planner from the coffee table to beside her, a few pictures fell out of it. Mayank could make out that they were her portfolio snaps.

"Your portfolio snaps?"

"Yeah, actually, a friend of mine from Delhi who has shifted here and works with UTV had asked for them."

These pictures came as a surprise for Revathi.

"Wow, you're into modeling? That's great! How come Mayank you never told me about it?"

116

"I must have forgotten. By the way, Rewa, Revathi's husband is turning TV producer and very soon he is shooting a pilot. So perhaps, you could try your luck with him."

"Really? What's the serial?"

"Oh, it's just got approved actually but it's a very exciting subject…" Before Revathi could say anything more, Mayank cut her short.

"Oh, come on Revathi, you call it exciting? It's so clichéd." He turned to Rewa. "You know what, it is about a husband and a wife, who are going through the normal set of problems that couples do after about seven or eight years of marriage. And in this scenario, the wife's jilted lover, who is now materially successful but emotionally bankrupt resurfaces in their life…and the rest you know."

"Hey, but that's an interesting subject."

Rewa's endorsement of the subject surprised Mayank.

"What, does it really appeal to you?"

"Of course, it does. Your first love is perhaps the most beautiful feeling that anybody experiences. Now if for some reason it doesn't fructify into marriage but comes right back into your life at a point when your marriage has touched its nadir, it really carries such huge scope for drama."

Mayank sounded least impressed. Revathi chipped in.

"Okay, tell me, have you guys seen this movie, Raincoat? How did you find it?"

"I found it superb. Amazingly sensitively written and made and with terrific realistic performances."

"And you Mayank?"

"It was crap."

Revathi found the discordant notes between them quite intriguing. Were their differences so pronounced on other matters that were more important for conjugal existence as well, she wondered? She hoped they weren't. Mayank, in his subconscious self, had not taken particularly well to Rewa's open expression of her likes that were nearly alienating for him.

"But tell me, why do such subjects appeal so much to you?"

Rewa was taken off guard by the directness of this question, as she realized that her answer could possibly open up many other questions, at least, in Mayank's mind, if not outside it. She knew this much from whatever understanding she had of Mayank. She knew he could be very conservative, even seeming suspicious. She did not feel sure about what to say.

"Well, I wouldn't know really. I guess it's a question of one's sensibilities."

Mayank's first query, though blunt, had by no means prepared her for what he was getting at.

"Okay, tell me, have you been in a relationship?"

This was a subject on which Rewa wouldn't have minded talking privately. But in front of Revathi, she found it awkward. Mayank, himself, within moments realized the absurdity of it. Perhaps, Revathi had got used to his casual impertinence but for Rewa there was still some way to go to get used to it. Besides, for Rewa to face up to such a situation in front of another woman would have called for even greater preparation.

"Yes, I have been in love. I was in a relationship for four long years. We broke off last year."

Mayank's reaction was more of shock, Revathi's was of awe. With that one statement of Rewa's, Revathi knew that Rewa was a much stronger woman than Mayank or she would have imagined. She perhaps had immense conviction and clarity in thought – something Mayank himself seemed to be lacking. After all, for a woman, on the verge of her marriage, to admit of her past so unambiguously and in front of another woman, was reflective of an honest character, she felt. Revathi only wished that she was not a part of this conversation between Mayank and Rewa. There was no way she could possibly have slipped out either.

Mayank realized that it was best if he buried the subject at that. He had been impulsive, even stupid to rake it up in the first place. He was in any case trying hard not to look normal after Rewa's confession. Seeing Mayank's expression, Rewa had a fair idea of what could have been going inside Mayank's mind. Mayank would perhaps be hoping that she wouldn't have screwed up with someone else too, other than this solitary ex-boyfriend of hers. Rewa knew from a survey that she had done as part of her curriculum that though most men had had sexual encounters before their marriage, somewhere, in their heart of hearts they always desired their wives to be virgins. Though a majority of men sampled for this study belonged to smaller towns, Rewa knew that the story was the same with men all across.

Over coffee, another interesting topic came up for discussion. Revathi saw a copy of Mid Day lying on the adjoining table. The cover story had an opinion poll of Mumbaiities on the issue of what they felt the rightful solution to Gudiya's fiasco.

Well, Gudiya was an ill-fated lady in Haryana. Once married to a soldier serving in the army, her husband went missing in the Kargil War. Even after four years when her husband did not return, he was assumed dead and subsequently Gudiya entered into a second marriage. Now her first husband, who had been assumed dead, had suddenly resurfaced and wanted to have her back. But the twist in the tale was that Gudiya at this point, was into the eighth month of pregnancy from her second husband. What had made the fiasco more contentious was the manner in which the matter was sorted out in an impromptu Panchayat organized and telecast live by a news channel.

The picture of Gudiya on the tabloid's cover evoked a reaction from Revathi.

"What Gudiya had to go through was so unfortunate. I mean, as a woman I can sense the predicament she'd have been in. And then this channel makes a mockery of the whole exercise."

Rewa added to Revathi's observation.

"Yes, what's even worse is that she eventually had to dump the person who stood by her in her worst phase. I doubt if a woman would do that unless coerced."

Rewa's observation surprised Mayank yet again.

"But you only said that it's virtually impossible to get over your first love. Perhaps she loved only her first husband. It's possible that the second marriage was just a compromise."

"Yes, Mayank, but even that compromise entailed a certain responsibility. How can a woman dump her man after bearing his child in her womb for eight months? Do you have any idea what that man would have gone through?"

Rewa appeared anguished when she said this, but Mayank was quietly enjoying her mini outburst. Mayank's provocation, after all, was only for the effect. He actually wanted to see her react to it. And her reaction had definitely made him feel somewhat reassured. He gathered that Rewa did have an innate sense of responsibility in her. Mayank concluded from it that while Rewa valued her first love immensely, post marriage her sense of commitment would ensure that she is always loyal to her husband. There was a method to Mayank's madness.

Mayank saw a pensive look on Revathi's face; he gathered that she too would have made her notes which they could discuss later and make a more conclusive assessment of Rewa. After the coffee session, Revathi took leave and in accordance with a pre-decided plan, Mayank was now supposed to show Rewa around Mumbai. He wished like a kid, though, that Revathi would be there with them.

≈

Mayank and Rewa spent most part of that evening at and around the Gateway of India. They took a boat ride that took them into the heart of the sea. The motorboat that must have had a seating capacity of about forty people also seated around fifteen of them on chairs laid on its roof. Rewa and Mayank were the lucky ones to have managed to get a place on top.

Rewa enjoyed the trip thoroughly. From a point in the middle of the sea when she looked around, the distant glittering lights of the city looked majestic. They looked like the stars do, when viewed from land. Mayank, however, appeared restrained and even a bit preoccupied. Rewa wondered what was it that had made him immune to all the excitement that everybody else over there was experiencing. She gathered that perhaps it must have been the work pressure. After all, he had bunked office to be with her.

"Hey, Mayank, look into the camera; this view looks out of this world." Rewa went on the other side and clicked Mayank's picture with a rock in the background.

"What happened, Mayank? Is something bothering you?"

"No, no, just had to make an important call to office. Unfortunately there is no signal in this part."

Rewa tried empathizing with Mayank.

"I understand, Mayank. Marketing must be a tough job, nah? One of my friends is into ad-sales with The Indian Express in Delhi. I tell you, her weekly targets make her go crazy."

Mayank only faintly nodded to give the impression that he was there. In reality, he was feeling a strange forlornness; he tried hard not to delve into what was causing it.

By the time the boat journey ended, it was almost time for dinner. Though they deliberated on a couple of eating options, Mayank made sure they opted for Tendulkars' coz he remembered that an ICC trophy match between India and Pakistan that was being played at Lords would be at its final stages. Though Rewa quite abhorred cricket, she didn't mind going with Mayank's choice for once; after all, post-marriage compromises would in any case have to become the order of the day, she thought. Another reason why Mayank was tempted to try out Tendulkars' today was because he remembered an advertisement of the restaurant in the Mumbai Times that morning that offered a 50% flat discount to all customers in case India won.

But Tendulkars' turned out to be one crazy experience. When they reached there, the atmosphere was already festively chaotic. At least three Tendulkar look-alikes could be spotted instantly. Two of them were the hotel attendants and the third, an over enthusiastic guest. Even as the match was shown on a wall screen, all three took their turns to be the cheerleaders for the Indian team. And this, mind you was ironical considering that the real Tendulkar had pulled out of the match due to a tennis elbow injury.

Rewa found the whole ambience murderous for any intimate interaction. Mayank, on the other hand, got sucked into it almost naturally. What added to Rewa's woes was a thoroughly intriguing menu card that gave her absolutely no idea of what to opt for. Most of the items, for example were pre-fixed with cricketing jargons. Hence, she had to choose from Square Cut Butter Nans, Reverse Sweep Chicken Biryani, Forward Short Leg Boneless Chicken, Flipper Veg Hyderabadi and the like.. She found it irritating. Unable to make up their minds, they instead ordered for just the soup in order to bide more time to decide.

Rewa's aversion for cricket went back to 1986. The last ball six that Javed Miandad had hit off Chetan Sharma had completely shaken her confidence in India's cricketing prowess and somehow it remained that way since. Once again, now a pall of gloom had descended upon the restaurant; Pakistan seemed to have an upper hand. Surprisingly for Rewa, Mayank was so consumed in the game that he seemed completely out of elements now.

"Bloody hell, he's been the captain for four years now and yet doesn't know a thing about bowling changes. Oh, man, get Sehwag to bowl of couple of overs and he'll do the trick."

Another cricket enthusiast, seated on an adjoining table with an equally disinterested looking wife joined in.

"India can't do a thing without Tendulkar. Look how they play like school boys."

Mayank took it upon himself to reply back.

"But what has it got to do with Tendulkar I don't understand. It's the defeatist body language mind you. Look at Laxman. I'm sure when the opposition sees his sloppy movements they know this is a team of losers."

In barely a few moments, everybody, including each of the Tendulkar look-alikes was voicing his opinion on what had gone wrong. Rewa wondered how easily opinion was available in this country, at any place or time and on any subject. One fanatic, who looked inebriated as well, raised a near war cry. "Dravid lao, desh bachao" he kept shouting. They later discovered that the political flavor in his sloganeering was not without reason. He was a small time Shiv Sena leader.

Barely had they finished with their soup that Rewa quite firmly decided they were not going to waste any more time in the Tendulkars. She virtually staged a walk out. Mayank followed suit, sensing he did not have much of an option. Still unable to decide where to eat and with the confusion prolonging, Mayank got a cab, got into it with Rewa and almost impulsively asked the driver to take them to the Juhu Beach. It took them an hour's drive to reach the spot.

On arriving there, he led Rewa straight to a Paratha stall that had its seating arrangement made on the beach in open air. Rewa for once loved the ambience. The freshness of the sea breeze soothed her ruffled tempers. Both of them actually made full use of the "unlimited" option available to them and gorged as many different varieties of the parathas that they could. An ice-cream, a small 200ml cold drink and a mineral water bottle were complimentary along with the parathas. And to top it all, the entire package came for a meager 65 bucks.

Post dinner they took a stroll on the beach. Luckily enough it was a full moon night and the tides were more active than their normal dead state.

Rewa went into her vivacious best, cracking jokes almost every time at Mayank's expense. Mayank realized that she was perhaps more intelligent than what he had imagined her to be. At least, she was far more presentable and sensible compared to many any other girls he had met. Was it then a chauvinistic psyche that had made him wary of her? He wondered. After all, Rewa's extroverted nature and near crazy sense of humor were in sharp contrast with his intense persona. Unlike her, it always took Mayank a long time to break the ice with people.

On their walk down the beach, Rewa surprised Mayank with her knowledge of English phonetics, correcting almost every sentence he spoke. Mayank had this habit of beginning most of his sentences with, "Actually…" and every time he would say that, he would be reprimanded by Rewa. "'Actually' isn't a correct way to begin the sentence, instead begin the sentence with 'Look'…" Mayank absorbed it meekly enough. These admonishments, however, made Mayank really conscious when he spoke.

Rewa gave him a list of words to pronounce and corrected his pronunciation of each of these words. It was a baffling experience for Mayank as he had never heard any of his friends pronounce the words thus. He had a particularly tough time pronouncing "renaissance". Rewa, on the other hand, seemed to have great fun being his tutor. Mayank, after a while, quite enjoyed being tutored thus. He realized that a tutor-pupil equation had its own undercurrent of romance.

And then they reached a point, when Rewa suddenly looked like she was struck by some unhappy memory. Rewa looked pensively into the sea and nearly switched off from the conversation.

"What's the matter, Rewa? Is everything okay?"

"Yeah… yeah…all's well." Rewa tried skirting the matter at first. But Mayank's persistence eventually made her confess the true reason.

"Around three years ago, we'd come here on a college excursion. It was right at this point that Mahesh had proposed to me."

Mayank was zapped to hear this at a point when he had just about begun to feel romantic about her. It looked like Rewa was still affected by her past or else she'd have had the prudence to avoid the mention of it; he thought. Rewa too realized the folly of what she had said, almost immediately.

"I'm sorry Mayank, I just got carried away."

Mayank did not know what to say. There was an awkward moment between them till Mayank did something more awkward. In an impulse, he brought himself close to Rewa, held her face with his hands and gave her a delicate cute peck on her lips. It took a while before the feel of the kiss sank into her. Rewa reciprocated. Encouraged, Mayank shifted gears and soft pecks gave way to passionate smooching; and he did it right in the open, completely oblivious of some urchins and a couple of eunuchs observing them.

And then, Mayank realized why he was enjoying the act so thoroughly. He had been imagining he was kissing Revathi.

Mayank returned home at nearly two in the morning. He lay in bed for sometime thinking about all that had happened during the day. There were only two sentences of Rewa that prominently stood out in his memory. One had Rewa confessing to being in a relationship and the other one of Rewa telling him about Mahesh having proposed to her on the Juhu beach. Mayank felt quite rattled thinking about it. From all the interaction that he had with her during the day, he was unable to form any definite opinion about her. But there was one thing he was pretty sure about: Rewa would never cease to surprise him with newer aspects of her persona. While a majority of these surprises were expected to be positive ones, a few hiccups could not be ruled out.

Mayank felt a desperate urge to exchange notes with Revathi on the matter. But with the clock reading 2:30am, he restrained himself from calling her. He instead settled for a somewhat weird SMS, which he couldn't help forwarding, on the spur of the moment. It read: *'All desirable things in life are banned, illegal, fattening or already married.'*

A day after, Mayank and Revathi met for a while in the evening at the Woodlands Garden Café in Juhu. Mayank's supposed agenda was a discussion on Rewa. Rewa, though still in town, had to keep her date with her uncle's family as there was a small function in the house.

"Look Mayank, instead of raising doubts about her commitment, I feel you must appreciate the fact that Rewa has been brutally honest with you," Revathi opined.

"Revathi, Revathi, I'm not doubting her commitment."

"Then why are you letting yourself be bothered unnecessarily about her past which you know is a closed chapter?"

Mayank felt quite helpless about Revathi not being able to understand his state of mind. And then he blurted out the obvious.

"Okay, now, let me be brutally honest like Rewa. Fact is that no matter how broadminded I may project myself my psyche is no different from that of most typical Indian males. Yes, it rattles me that my wife has been in a relationship for four long years."

Revathi was stunned by the raw truth of the statement. A convoluted male psyche was something she had herself quietly experienced at some stage. The situation made her go back the memory lane as she remembered Pranav confessing to her in one of their initial nights after marriage, that one of the reasons why he had been so smitten by her was because she was 'pristine'. He wanted to be the first recipient of her love.

Revathi went on the defensive mode as she could only reason out with Mayank.

"Mayank, I feel you should be more pragmatic. I mean what's the difference between a male or a female today, when it comes to exposure to different situations. What if Rewa has the same expectation from you?"

"But Revathi, there's one more problem." Mayank complained, almost sounding childlike, ensconced in Revathi's company.

"Now what's that?"

"She is not as beautiful as you."

If another man had said a thing like that, Revathi would have become wary of his motives. Revathi liked propriety to be honored. She didn't exactly know why she had made an exception for Mayank. After all, she had been indulgent enough to let Mayank get away with a remark like that. Perhaps it had to do with women wanting to be flirted with by men, who were 'safe' in their perception, she thought. Besides, Mayank always enjoyed the advantage of the affection his innocent impertinence had won from Revathi. Revathi realized that in this case, his behavior was getting weirder.

Later that evening, in accordance with a pre-decided plan, Revathi accompanied Mayank to a Saree Emporium nearby. Mayank's mother had called up from Indore and instructed him to gift Rewa a saree. And since he had no idea about sarees, Mayank had to again turn to his trouble shooter to help him out.

Revathi selected a sober chikan saree that she felt Rewa could use for wearing both at home and office. Rewa was scheduled to leave for Delhi the next morning.

Once the saree had been purchased, Mayank traveled in Revathi's car till Andheri. Due to heavy traffic, the small distance nearly an hour to cover. And the time gave Mayank another opportunity to blurt out one of his myriad feelings.

"You know Revathi, sometimes I feel the problem lies with me. I mean my expectations from life are too high, I guess. I'm surprised that after college, which is almost eight years now I haven't fallen in love with a girl my age."

When Mayank spoke, the sheer comfort that he shared with Revathi made his body language go haywire. On the rear seat that he shared with Revathi, he had actually bent low, leaning towards Revathi in a very casual manner. His head was only barely an inch away from finding solace on Revathi's shoulder. It did not escape Revathi's attention but the seriousness of the discussion made her ignore it.

Revathi wondered though what he meant when he said he hadn't fallen in love with a girl his age. Was he implying that he had fallen in love with her? She thought for a moment and then almost instantly concluded that she was allowing her imagination to be stretched too far. As usual she played Agony Aunt with precision for the remainder of the journey.

That evening, however, of all people it was a comment from her chauffeur that upset Revathi.

"Madam, don't mind me saying this... choti mooh, badi baat, but somehow I don't like this man..."

When Revathi, rattled by this unprovoked remark from her driver, made him speak out what he was getting at, he explained thus: "Iss aadmi ki niyat mujhe theek nahi lagti. Yeh har waqt aapse chipakna chahta hai..." (I don't think this man's intentions are okay. He always tries to get physically close with you.) The directness of the driver's observations shook Revathi out of her senses. The chauffeur, on the other hand, defended his concern with the clichéd statement that he had consumed her salt and could never see anything wrong happening to her...

Even a few hours later, Revathi kept thinking about what the chauffeur had told her. After all, for a person like her chauffeur to show the courage to speak to her thus, indicated that the matter had indeed reached a stage where it could no longer escape public censure. Moreover it also led Revathi onto introspection. Was Revathi being ethical in encouraging a relationship where the other person's unrestrained behavior would result in people raising their eyebrows?

That night, Revathi's sense of righteousness made her confess the incident to her husband. And to her shock, Pranav's reaction was not what she had been expecting.

"I knew it was coming. After all, if a guy can send a weird SMS like the one he did in the middle of the night, it is but obvious that his behavior in front of you will be that much more aggressive."

"Pranav, but I'm sure he doesn't do these things intentionally. I guess he is just impulsive and innocent."

"He is impulsive but not in the least innocent. But yes, he exploits your innocence to the hilt."

"What do you mean, Pranav?"

"Look Revathi, you must have had the best intentions in helping Mayank buy a saree for Rewa. But have you ever thought what an acquaintance who sees you do that will think?"

Revathi was in a bit of a quandary.

"You're perhaps right, Pranav. I will speak to Mayank and ask him to exercise more caution."

Pranav's diatribe made Revathi think the whole night about the way Mayank had behaved lately. She realized that his dependence on her had indeed grown manifold, and this was ironical given that his own marriage was drawing closer.

Almost every second day now, Mayank would call her up and the conversations would stretch for at least half an hour. And on days when he did not call, Revathi would look slightly lost at the usual time at which he called, as if she expected his call. These conversations would normally take place at 10: 30 pm, a time that suited Revathi. It was a time when Revathi would normally be through with the day's chores and still have some time before hitting the bed. What really bugged Pranav was that Mayank would go on prolonging these conversations by eventually making them venture into areas that should, by cogent parameters, have had nothing of interest for him.

Revathi realized that she would have to do something to discourage this dependence, especially since it was really unwarranted.

Mayank had a long telephonic chat with Rewa that night. He realized that while talking to any sweet female gave him a high, Rewa was unable to get into his mind the way Revathi could. For instance, his attempts at discussing his future career plans did not quite evoke the sort of empathy and synergy that he was now wont to expect in Revathi. If not anything else, Revathi made a good listener. Or maybe, to give Rewa the benefit of doubt, he felt that she was perhaps too young to be a good listener. Her enthusiasm always made her that much more excited to spell out her own agenda.

Much after the chat, Mayank remained awake. He wanted to continue the absorbing discussion that he had with Revathi early during the day. In another few minutes, this urge became unquenchable and though he dithered for a while, he ended up calling her up at about a quarter past twelve, assuming wishfully that she would be awake.

Mayank's call caught Revathi at a wrong time. Pranav and she were making love. Pranav, in fact, was trying hard to hold back orgasm so that he could prolong the experience. This was when the pleasure got spoiled by the ringing of Revathi's mobile. Revathi found it absurd to see Mayank's number at such an odd hour. Pranav found it frustrating. He took the cell in his hand and was about to cut the call when Revathi took it away.

"It must be something urgent," reasoned Revathi even as Pranav looked irritated. She took the call.

"Yeah, Mayank?" Revathi sounded curt.

"Revathi, hi, I hope you were awake." Mayank missed out on the curtness or perhaps ignored it.

"Yeah, tell me."

"Revathi, I wanted to discuss something important. Well, actually you were right. I realize I shouldn't be bothered about Rewa's past. I realize I should disband this regressive male psyche that has two different sets of norms for men and women."

"It's good you've realized it. I'm happy for you."

Revathi hoped that the conversation would end with that. After all Pranav was in an extremely awkward situation. He was watching some hot stuff on FTV, just to retain his momentum and looked upset.

But Mayank went on: "But Revathi, I just had a long chat with her just now and I still have apprehensions that we are two different people. I mean she was not able to relate at all with my aspirations. She is a complete conformist. I doubt if she will be of support to me in my ambitions."

"Look Mayank, you are again being very finicky. How can you do so many flip flops on your opinion about her? More than reflecting any inability on her part, it shows that you are thoroughly confused."

Pranav, by now, looked extremely agitated. He was making all sorts of gestures and even calling out for Revathi in hushed tone to quickly end the conversation. Mayank did sense some commotion on the other side but chose to ignore it. Revathi took the cue from Pranav and tried her bit, but in vain.

"Mayank, can we talk about this when we meet?"

"Okay, I guess these things cannot be discussed properly over phone."

Revathi once again believed that the conversation would end and once again she was mistaken. For Mayank's digressions in order to keep the conversation going were yet to show up.

"By the way, how is your new servant doing? I hope she doesn't bunk that much."

From experience Mayank knew that the servant was one topic that Revathi could always speak on at length.

"They're all the same, Mayank. This one has come with a new problem. I caught her red-handed cozying up to my driver on the rear seat of our car. Just imagine what people would have thought."

Mayank actually wondered why she faced such problems both on professional front as well as with her personal staff. Was she too soft so as to be taken for a ride? Or did she actually trust people to the point that they ditched her?

"Well, I've heard of an agency that supplies servants and takes guarantee…"

"You mean the one at Santa Cruz?"

By now Revathi did not seem that keen to wind up the talk.

"Yeah, I guess it's at Santa Cruz. I know of it because Vishal has got his maid from there."

"Okay, I'll try them out. Thanks, Mayank for this."

The unending conversation now tested Pranav's patience. Pranav eventually walked out of the room in disgust.

"And did you sort out with Reliance the problem you had of faulty billing?"

"Yeah, in fact, I'm thinking of going back to Hutch."

"In that case, go for the scheme I told you– the one in which you make cell to cell calls for just 30paise."

"Okay, in fact, I'll call you tomorrow and take the details of it."

By the time the conversation ended a good twenty minutes had gone by. Pranav walked back into the room and looked dispassionate.

"I'm so sorry, Pranav. He went on and on. Come, let's get on…"

"To hell with you! If you don't support his stupid interactions, he can never go on and on." Pranav blew a fuse, shocking her with the intensity.

"Pranav, now forget it."

"I mean what does he have to do with how your servant is performing? Why does he have to worry about your mobile bill? Am I not there? I'm telling you, this guy is a manipulator; he is employing mind games to make you depend upon him. And you are just enjoying being pampered."

As long as Pranav's outburst had to do with his craving for Revathi's time and attention, it went off well with Revathi. But when Pranav hinted at Mayank's guile, she couldn't but hit back, because it indirectly meant that Revathi was a fool to not see through Mayank.

"At least, he's not as mean as Sonal," she finally retorted in anger. "He doesn't concoct reasons to have me out for dinner."

Pranav looked zapped by this reaction.

"Now you better not get Sonal into the picture. She has never called when we've been making love."

"That's because we hardly ever do it."

Pranav was stunned to hear this. Revathi's last sentence said so much about their relationship lately.

It led to a bigger flare up between the couple till Revathi promised not to take Mayank's call if ever he called again at such time. After wasting a lot of time, they finally got down to completing the unfinished task. They made love. Pranav's protests were thus silenced for the time being, not that he was convinced. He just went through the motions this time round and ejaculated soon enough. Pranav knew that no matter what Revathi projected, perhaps even without her realizing it, she was far too preoccupied with Mayank and his problems.

The next evening Mayank had just returned to office after seeing off Rewa when Revathi called him. Revathi was uncharacteristically terse and business like. After exchanging pleasantries and enquiring about Rewa, she did some serious talking this time

"Mayank, from now on we'll have to reduce our conversations. As an exercise, unless if it is urgent, let's not talk with each other before say every third day. We'll talk preferably at around 10:30pm and try and not prolong the conversation beyond ten minutes."

Revathi did not encourage a prolonged conversation and hung up once she had made her point.

That night, Mayank wondered what could have led Revathi to formulate the code of conduct between them. It surely wasn't her brainchild. He related it with Rewa asking him about their friendship just before her train left for Mumbai. Though Rewa tried her best to make her query look as normal as possible, it couldn't hide the fact that their friendship did not give a very normal perception to people.

On introspection, Mayank accepted that Revathi had become an inescapable habit for him, just like chocolates do become for kids beyond a point. And just like parents limit their kids' consumption of chocolates, Pranav wanted Mayank to have less of Revathi from now on. After all, Mayank of late had wanted to talk to her and be her with all the time. So long as he was single, there was no one to watch over him and check him even if he went overboard. But for Revathi who had a family, things must have got really difficult; he empathized.

Mayank clung to his pillow and tried sleeping. In his half sleepy state he imagined the pillow to be Rewa and wondered how Rewa would be on bed. In the morning when he woke up by the ringing of his cell phone, he realized he had been dreaming about Revathi.

10

Cupid Hath Struck

"Wah shakl pighli to har shay mein dhal gayee jaise...
ajeeb baat hui hai use bhulane mein"- Javed Akhtar, in Tarkash

Asemblance of propriety seemed to have been finally restored in the equations that Mayank and Revathi shared. Mayank was still reeling from the shock of the code of conduct handed over to him by Revathi. In the last eight days or so they had not spoken. Not that it was easy for Mayank to resist that but he chose to play safe. He feared being snubbed by Revathi if he called. He would perhaps have not been able to take that from someone who had given him the liberty to call her anytime.

Mayank had sent an SMS though, asking "How are you, ma'am?" Revathi had replied. "Fine, thanks. Hope you too are well." Revathi's ignoring the term "ma'am" and 'hoping' that Mayank was well hadn't left him with scope to reply. It was not a question but a deliberate assumption, after all.

It happened to be the second Saturday of the month and Mayank was home. Being a Saturday, he lay in bed listlessly and scanned through some property ads in the newspaper. He wanted to invest in a new house that Rewa and he would be staying in after marriage; to that end he had even planned to go and see a house at Mindspace in Malad.

At around noon, he got a call on his cell. Surprisingly enough, it was Revathi. For a moment, when he saw her name flashing on his cell phone screen, he did not know how to react. It was strange that the call that would make him jump in excitement now made him nearly tremble. He feared that there may have been more problem between husband and wife due to his last SMS. Mayank didn't exactly know why this fear lurked in his mind. On introspection, he realized that the fear was perhaps generated by his own feeling of guilt. After all, Mayank had in a way, known or unknown, been an intruder into Revathi's life. Even as Mayank ruminated, after about a dozen rings, the cell phone stopped ringing. Mayank called her back.

"What happened, Mayank? Why weren't you taking the call?' Revathi sounded very normal.

"I'm sorry… I was in the bath…"

"Mayank can you tell me where IP Colony is… actually I'm on the Link Road at Borivali."

"What?" Mayank was stunned to know that she was barely a kilometer away from his house.

"Yeah, actually, my colleague Prabhakar has been down with a lung ailment. I had come to see him but since I don't know the way, I thought I'd check out with you."

Mayank gave her the direction and almost in the same vein cajoled her to drop in at his place for a while once she was through with Prabhakar.

"Please, Revathi, I want to talk… just for a few minutes."

"Okay, I'll try…"

"No, you won't try… You will have to come for me. I'm paging you my address."

Revathi wondered why she could never say a blunt 'no' to Mayank. Had it been any other man instead of Mayank, she was dead sure she wouldn't have entertained him. But in Mayank's case there was something in him that made her treat him differently. Revathi didn't exactly know whether it was his maturity that made him talk to her at the same level like a person, much beyond his age or it was this childish, affectionate cajoling that was sometimes akin to the way Ria behaved. She surmised it was perhaps the unusual dichotomy of both that Mayank had in him.

A couple of hours went by. It was a half past one now and Mayank had given up whatever faint hope he had of seeing Revathi. At least she would have called, if she intended to, he felt sure. Right then, the doorbell rang. Mayank was surprised to see Revathi standing there. Revathi smiled.

"Hey."

For a while, Mayank did not utter a word. He had had a whisky peg last night of a rather unknown brand. He wondered, for a moment, if the drink was manifesting its effect now.

"Hi."

"Surprised? I'm sure you weren't expecting me."

"Well, yes. I wasn't. I thought you'd have left. Come"

"I thought I'll drop in for a while but then since I was coming for the first time, I thought I'll get something for you."

Revathi took out a packet of an imported Cadbury chocolate from her purse.

"You think I eat chocolates?"

"Well, normally kids do, so I thought you would."

This piece of leg-pulling, which Revathi only sparingly resorted to, eased the situation, and within minutes they opened up to sharing developments like they normally did.

Revathi was now seated on the thick gadda in Mayank's drawing room, sipping the lemon tea that Mayank was so good at preparing. Revathi realized, though, that Mayank was not his normal self. The absence of conversation in the last few days had apparently left him upset and like a kid, he couldn't conceal the pout that revealed his emotion.

"Mayank, are you okay? Haven't I obeyed you and come to your place."

"No, I'm not upset. I'm glad you have come."

"Then would you bother to look a bit cheerful if that's not asking for too much?"

Mayank conjured up a sheepish grin. Something kept bothering him though.

"Revathi, is your husband okay about our relationship?"

The suddenness and bluntness of the query took Revathi by surprise. Revathi for a moment did not feel too comfortable about the use of the term, 'relationship'. She'd have been more comfortable if it had been substituted with friendship. But strangely, Revathi did not protest, which made Mayank believe that she was accepting the truth; that theirs was not a normal friendship. It had nothing abnormal in it either, except that both cared for each other, much more than what a man and a woman in their respective positions would.

"Why do you ask me that?"

"Look Revathi, if I am the cause of any friction between you and your husband, then I should know. Otherwise, it will only complicate matters."

"But what makes you feel that you are a cause?"

"Revathi, I may have known you only for the last few months but I know you well enough to know that the code of conduct that you spelt out was not your brainchild."

One of the factors that Revathi had always liked about Mayank was his propensity to face truth in its most disconcerting forms; that too head on. This was precisely what he was doing now but somehow she did not like being put in the situation. Revathi wished she could talk as freely to Mayank about her husband's problems and those that had to do with Sonal, just the way Mayank bared his heart to her.

"The problem is bigger than you think it to be. It's... forget it." Revathi checked herself, realizing that her sense of responsibility did not allow her to divulge her marital problems to another man.

Mayank had a fair idea of what Revathi might have wanted to say.

"What is it Revathi?" He probed.

"Look Mayank, you understand everything. Then, why don't you just accept the situation the way it is. I mean, if Pranav feels a bit uncomfortable about our friendship, you must understand his perspective also."

Mayank knew that Revathi had cleverly steered clear of revealing the 'bigger problem'. He admired her for this.

"Does he trust you?"

"Look Mayank, you understand everything. Then, why don't you just accept the situation the way it is. I mean, if Pranav feels a bit uncomfortable about our friendship, you must understand his perspective also."

"Does he trust you?"

"Of course! It's not a question of trust. Well, how do I put it? Look, if you were in his position you would realize that no dignified man would want his wife to be 'controlled' by another man."

"Controlled?"

"Yes, I mean, he doesn't like you advising me on things that concern my life. He doesn't like me sharing so much about my life with you."

Mayank just listened and tried to absorb what he heard.

"And that I feel is justified to an extent. He feels every relationship should have a name and that your friendship with me is a confused relationship."

Mayank just listened.

"And to some extent, I tend to agree with Pranav. He can't be so wrong about me."

Mayank took a deep breath before be finally spoke.

"Okay, so how do we sort out this confusion? I have an idea. I'll tell you what you are to me and then you tell me what I am to you. We'll try to give a name to our bond."

Revathi found it a little odd but did not protest as she anticipated what Mayank would say next.

"Look Revathi, I need you," Mayank began and then took a pause. He said this in a somewhat intriguing lovelorn tenor; as if there was something he wanted Revathi to read from his tenor. Revathi on the other hand, had got quite used to Mayank's knack for creating subtle confusion in their interactions. It did register to her at times that this was perhaps a safe form of flirting that Mayank indulged in. However, the ambivalence in his manner prevented her from reacting in any conclusive way, lest Mayank retracted with a 'just kidding' kind of muse.

"Okay, to be honest you are a need for me. I need you as a friend who I can freely interact with on anything. It eases me of all my worries and makes me feel so unencumbered. Besides, I need to meet you also say once in about ten days. I somehow feel very confident, protected and carefree when you are around," Mayank went on.

Revathi heard it out intently, even though she looked more and more obfuscated. Mayank, after all, had subtly made an additional demand on her, to meet once every ten days.

"Revathi, I'm grateful to you for the support that you've given me. But you'll have to be this much more accommodating towards my need for interacting and meeting you more often. You will have to do this for me till I get married."

Mayank's words were a clear reflection of the fact that he sought the emotional solace in Revathi, which by all means he ought to have in Rewa.

As Mayank said this, he almost naturally got off the chair and put his head on her lap. Revathi did not know what it implied, yet it somehow did not look that unnatural for her to protest. She wondered why. Perhaps the conversation had set the mood for such a gesture.

Revathi found the feel of Mayank's head or her lap a bit awkward. Mayank, for his part was quietly relishing the feel of Revathi's thighs. But when Mayank looked directly into her eyes from that unusual proximity, it nearly made her squirm.

"Revathi, why don't you wear sarees?" Mayank asked with yet another flash of directness that only he was capable of.

Almost instantly he also realized how odd it may have seemed. "I mean, it will look really nice on you," he tried to justify.

Revathi still looked unsure in her reaction. Mayank chose to quickly change the topic.

"Okay, now you tell me what I am to you."

Revathi thought before she spoke.

"An immature kid who always sulks and wants attention. Mayank, will you please sit there?"

Mayank at once got up and took his old seating position, realizing that Revathi had finally protested.

"Actually, I'm sorry…"

Revathi ignored him in order to safely deviate from any embarrassment. A glint suddenly surfaced in her eyes and she seemed to have remembered something.

"Hey, you have to congratulate me."

"For what?"

"I forgot to tell you. I'm getting the AD World award for the best Brand Manager of the year. "

"Really?"

"Yeah, I just got to know of it last night."

"Congrats!"

For some strange reason, Mayank's reaction was rather mellowed.

"They're planning to give away the awards at the Taj Lands End on 30th. In fact I'll try and arrange a pass for you and you must come."

Mayank nodded.

Another ten minutes went by.

"Hey, I think I should leave now. I came here for 10 minutes and it's almost 40."

"Does Pranav know that you've come here?"

"Yeah, I mean I'd called him and said so… why?"

"No, nothing. Anyway, which way are you going?"

"I think I'll take the Link Road."

"Great."

Mayank persuaded her to come with him to Mindspace in Malad, where he was supposed to scout for his new house. He was particularly keen to get her opinion on a flat that he had short listed. Though Revathi was not in the mood, Mayank's affectionate cajoling again made her budge. She agreed eventually, though 'for just 10 minutes'. In an instant afterthought, she added, "But make sure you behave yourself in front of my chauffeur." Mayank took the admonishment in his stride.

A few minutes later, Mayank led her into an eighth storey flat. Accompanying them was a surd property dealer. The dealer's expression couldn't hide his inquisitiveness to know whether Mayank and Revathi were husband and wife.

The flat in question, was a one bedroom-hall-kitchen apartment, popularly known as 1BHK in Mumbai's realty parlance. Revathi found it a little weird stepping in with Mayank to make a survey of the place, more so with the dealer looking at them in a probing way. About the only time that she was in a similar situation was when Pranav had led her into their Lokhandawala flat before finalizing the purchase. Mayank brimmed with excitement as he showed her around the house. She, somehow, did not want to cut his excitement short.

At the end of it, Mayank sought her opinion. And Revathi was back into avuncular mode.

"Mayank, it's a pretty decent flat but it has a small problem."

"What?'

"It opens towards the north. I'm not too sure but north is not considered an auspicious direction…ideally it should be east-west."

Mayank, at once let the flat go.

On her journey back home, Revathi somehow couldn't help feeling guilty. No, she had not done anything wrong but consciously or unconsciously, it was Mayank's indulgence that had begun to invite stares from people. He would behave as if they were a couple.

That night Revathi informed Pranav about her meeting with Mayank, in as much as it was a habit to tell her husband anything of consequence. Pranav's reaction, strangely, was one of resignation. It was as if he realized that Mayank couldn't be wished away so easily. Therefore, as long as he behaved prudently, Pranav might as well decide to come to terms with him.

A week went by in no time. It was the day of the AD World awards function. Revathi called up Mayank and informed him that she had got an invite for him that she would have it sent to him by a peon.

After this conversation, Mayank found it tough to concentrate on work. He kept thinking about the evening and visualized Revathi walk up the podium to receive the award. Mayank imagined how the audience and the media would react. Would she make it to the next day's Mumbai Times or Mid-day?

That evening it rained heavily. As a result, Mayank reached the Taj Land's End almost an hour behind schedule. The small hall in which the Awards ceremony was taking place was jam packed by then. As a result he had to find himself a place at one of the side exits in the front. He didn't mind it though for the only moment for which he had arrived there was when Revathi would walk up the stage to take her award. Luckily for him, the award had not yet been given.

From where Mayank stood, he could see Revathi and Pranav

sitting in the second row from the front. A new addition on Revathi was a well shaped bindi that stood out and quite embellished her persona. Mayank, at once waved at-her. Revathi nodded with a guarded smile and then turned to look at the stage. Pranav, on the other hand gave a stare. Mayank realized within a moment what the stare was meant for. Mayank's jazzy shirt, un-tucked with the upper buttons left open, his hair uncombed and countenance unshaved, was not the way he'd have been expected to come for the occasion. Almost everyone present there was attired formally. Mayank hadn't bothered about the occasion. His sole focus after all was on Revathi.

The moment he had been waiting for finally arrived. Revathi went up on stage to receive the award. She got an outstanding applause from the audience. However, Mayank almost froze at the sight. Something was surely bothering him; he didn't exactly know what.

On quick introspection, he realized that there were two strong, though divergent emotions operating in him. On the one hand, he was happy for his friend, no doubt. But simultaneously he was also worried. He was worried that Revathi's success and the newer commitments that it would bring along, would further eat into the time and attention he had got used to expecting from her. Mayank realized that he was more worried than happy and felt stupid at his thought process going berserk. A headache added to the irritation.

That evening, even as Mayank craved for Revathi's attention, she was surely the cynosure of the media. She remained surrounded by about a half a dozen journalists, most of whom asked her some really unintelligent questions. Of course, she retained the patience to be irritated by them.

Mayank wondered if people would have given Revathi that

much importance if she was not pretty. Not that she got this award for being pretty but the fact that the winner looked stunningly beautiful surely turned that many more heads, he thought. Revathi was definitely the darling of the motley group of local media people assembled there. She was the woman of the moment.

Mayank restlessly walked across the hall, to and fro, looking constantly in Revathi's direction. His movement was rather wayward, but Mayank didn't seem to realize. Someone seeing him for the first time would even have got the impression that Mayank was on dope. He was hoping that Revathi would take notice and give him attention. Mayank was dying to talk to her. Revathi took notice, but pretended otherwise, as she found it dicey to indulge with him at that point. Instead, some of Revathi's colleagues from Shagun took notice and wondered what was cooking between them. Pranav found it embarrassing.

A little later it was time for photo-ops. Praful Deshpande, a renowned ad world guru and a charmer made good use of the opportunity. He got a photo clicked with Revathi, wherein he held a hand over her shoulder. Whether it was for the sake of political correctness or whatever, Revathi reciprocated, by formally putting her hand around his waist. The photographers were delighted; but Mayank anguished. He wondered if she would have got herself clicked with him in a similar pose. That it was not possible angered Mayank no end.

Mayank experienced some sort of frightening forlornness. Perhaps that Revathi was accessible to everybody, except him, in her moment of glory was what shook him completely.

A little later, when a couple of journalists just hung on, Mayank went and stood beside Revathi, as if to concretely register upon her that he had long been waiting for her attention. This gesture invited more stares. And Revathi helplessly wished that Mayank realized what he was doing. Pranav took the initiative and engaged Mayank in conversation, in an attempt to save Revathi of some embarrassment.

By the time Revathi was through with the media and thought of saying Hi to Mayank, she saw Mayank walking out in disarray. She was feeling hopelessly helpless about the entire episode. Pranav, in fact happened to overhear two journalists gossip. One wondered what Mayank's connection with Revathi was. The other related it with Revathi giving away a huge yearly deal to Mayank's sagging website; they put two and two together and inferred that Revathi and Mayank must be having an affair.

That night Pranav had a long chat with Revathi over Mayank.

"Look, after the way he behaved today, I'm quite sure he needs psychiatric help."

Revathi had nothing to say.

"I mean just think of the way he took those wild strides across the hall, the way he was dressed up and his callous body language. Believe me; he was behaving like a brooding, obsessed lover."

The words, *brooding, obsessed lover* dealt a nasty blow upon Revathi's ears and her conscience. Pranav probably would have dwelt a lot more on the subject if he did not have to shoot his pilot episode from the next morning. Much after Pranav had slept off, the impact of his words kept Revathi awake.

Mayank too couldn't sleep. The image of Praful and Revathi striking a pose for photographers kept him troubled all night. He felt more and more anguished as he thought of it. Between those images were the ones he hallucinated of being in Praful's place and giving Revathi a cute little peck on her cheeks even as the photographers made merry.

A flurry of grotesque, ill defined images feasted in Mayank's mind almost till morning. The headache too had intensified and added to his discomfiture. When Mayank woke up, his head was virtually crumbling with pain; he had never experienced anything like that before.

After taking in a couple of Saridon pills, he rushed to the Doctor. The Doctor was simply confounded to find that the BP had shot up to 160-100.

Mayank returned home aided by medicines. He was shaken by the BP reading and wondered if his emotional meandering had become such a major health detriment. Mayank was actually feeling scared about his condition. As in other such troubled situations, he thought of telling Revathi about it and ended up calling her.

Revathi's photograph with the award had appeared in the Mumbai Times that day. Pranav and Ria were celebrating her foray into Page 3 when she got this call from Mayank.

"Hi Mayank."

"Hi. Revathi I want to discuss something."

Revathi wondered what it could be other than congratulating her at this moment.

"Revathi my BP has shot up. It's 160-100..."

Revathi did not know what to say. After a pause, she finally spoke...

"Look, Mayank, don't get me wrong. For a while now, I've been feeling that you have not been behaving normal. And yesterday, it just got confirmed. I mean there was something very intriguing about the way you behaved; I mean your body language. It was just not normal, mind you. Something was just eating you from within."

Mayank heard her out, even as Revathi continued.

"Believe me, there is no shame in accepting a flaw. In fact, I would seriously recommend that you see a counselor."

At this point, Pranav intervened by telling Revathi that there was another call for her on the landline. And Revathi disconnected, saying she would call back. Mayank somehow did not find Revathi's words shocking or out of the blue. Instead, somewhere in his mind, he was perhaps glad that she was acknowledging the situation, the way it was. An unfounded optimism that Mayank might finally have his way with her was perhaps what kept him going.

Mayank waited for an hour but the call did not come. He then took a quick bath to make sure he wouldn't miss her call. Even by the time, he came out of the bathroom, wrapped in a bathing gown, Revathi had not called.

Mayank looked into the mirror. His eyes said it all. They looked obsessive and unflinchingly focused. He realized that he had never felt so passionate about a woman before.

Mayank threw the gown aside and gazed at himself. He imagined a bare Revathi emerge behind him and wrap him tight with both her hands. He closed his eyes and conjured up an aesthetic image of physical indulgence.

Mayank vaguely recalled that he had seen a picture in the early nineties of Boris Becker with a Black model, in a similar pose. It was for a campaign against apartheid. Itstruck him that his darkish skin contrasted with Revathi's fair one looked similar.

As Mayank stood in sheer abstraction, he couldn't escape the realization that every part of his corporeal entity was irresistibly yearning for Revathi. He had begun to love her. Cupid Hath Indeed Struck... and struck how!

11

A Fateful B' Day

Kabhi kissi ko mukammal jahan nahin milta,
Kahin zameen to kahin aasman nahin milta
Tere jahan mein aisa nahin ke pyar na ho,
Jahan umeed ho ootana wahan nahin milta...

- Nida Fazli

11th September happened to be Mayank's birthday. It would also have marked for him completing three months of knowing Revathi and of the sweet little bond that had formed between them. Ever since Mayank had started living away from his parents, he had thirsted for those special family dinners that unfailingly marked his birthday all his childhood years, even right up to the late teens. In the last nine years however, all he had to contend with was the company of friends with whom he enjoyed as much, but somehow did not feel as homely as he had begun to feel in Revathi's company. Perhaps a female could transport him to a different comfort zone, he thought.

It was not as if Mayank did not realize that his interest in Revathi had begun to border on obsession. After all, Mayank was intelligent and sensitive. He was equally aware that he was being unfair to

Rewa. Yet, he chose, and consciously so, not to curtail the free flow of natural emotion. By now, Mayank's predilection for Revathi was so pronounced that there was no way it could have escaped the notice of Vishal and Anil. Mayank, in his zest, had almost begun to ignore the fact that Revathi was a wife and a mother, apart from being his good friend.

"Look, the problem with you is that you've never really been intimate with any girl... *ek baar ladki ko kareeb se jaano to sabhi ladkiyaan ek si hoti hai...* (Once you know a girl closely, you will realize that all girls are similar)," explained Vishal, in his overconfident style.

Anil went a step further, "See, I can understand that you haven't felt the same way for someone before. But, that still doesn't justify such obsession with a married woman. And that too, when your own marriage is only months away. You have no idea of the mess that you are getting into."

Mayank, however, put forth his own reasoning for not putting the brakes on. 'The problem with modern life is that people are so devoid of true happiness that if a person does, with her sheer persona, bring in abundance, the simple joys of affection, care, camaraderie and togetherness, one does tend to overlook the ethical dilemmas inherent in the situation,' he reasoned.

On the 10th of September, Mayank called Revathi to book his date with her for his birthday.

"So can I expect you for dinner tomorrow at The Tantra in Andheri?"

"Well, meeting is not a problem but I would appreciate it very much if we can meet for lunch. Because, I want to be home with my family during dinner," Revathi replied in political correctness.

"But then, I would feel really lonely if you meet me during the day and leave me alone at dinner."

"Mayank, try and understand my position… "

"Isn't it possible that your husband and daughter join us?" Mayank clearly knew how to have his way. He knew perhaps that a joint meeting with Revathi and her husband would improve things and allow him to have more one-to-one meetings with Revathi in future.

Revathi took a pause. "Well, let me think. Let me, in fact speak to Pranav and get back to you."

Revathi for the first time was caught in an unusual dilemma that required her to keep "an outsider" happy at the expense of her own husband. She had also been feeling bad for Mayank's state and did not want to let him down on his birthday. This "outsider's" mention, on the other hand was enough to ruffle her husband by now.

Later that evening Revathi called up Mayank.

"Pranav has agreed to come." She sounded rather cryptic and added almost instantly. "So shall we meet tomorrow at The Poptates?"

"Poptates? Yeah, okay," nodded Mayank, rather faintly.

Mayank was a little surprised at the mention of Poptates. He did not, in particular like Continental or Italian food and Revathi was aware of it. Besides, he had in the last few weeks mentioned to her at least a couple of times that he wanted to try out The Tantra. Mayank didn't contradict her on the phone. He tended to realize that convincing Pranav to come out might have been difficult, in any case. Revathi sounded a bit uncertain during the conversation. And Mayank even thought that maybe she wanted to discuss something; but she quickly set aside her confusion and rounded off, almost abruptly. "See you tomorrow then."

Mayank woke up on his birthday, feeling upbeat, thanks to the numerous SMS messages that old friends had sent him at the stroke of midnight. The doorbell rang. Mayank opened the door to find a florist's guy standing there with a lovely bouquet for him. He grabbed it excitedly. He opened the envelope and read the Greeting Card. It read, "Hope you keep smiling and shining like this all year. Have a terrific birthday. Loads of Love, Rewa."

Mayank's excitement faded somewhat. He was expecting this bouquet to have come from Revathi. After all, he had sent one for her. An hour later, he got an SMS from Revathi. It read a terse "Happy B'day."

Later that evening, Mayank, Revathi, Pranav and Ria met at the appointed restaurant. Mayank tried being the perfect host, cracking jokes and being at his hospitable best. But within minutes he realized that something was amiss. It was apparent from his behavior that Pranav was presumably feeling out of place and had possibly been forced to come.

"So, how is your work going? Any progress with the serial?"

Pranav took a while to react and then spoke with conjured supremacy that couldn't hide his diffidence.

"Well, yes, only last week we shot our pilot episode and in another couple of days, it should be ready for presentation to the channel."

"Wow!! That's great. Congrats! "

"Thanks. In fact, let this project happen and lots will follow."

"Hmmm. Hmmm."

"Well, keep this to you- there's already an offer to tie-up with an American production house that wants to set up shop here. Should that happen we'll be unstoppable."

When Pranav said this, it was apparent from Revathi's initial reaction that she was not aware of the development. Revathi, in fact, was quietly wondering if her husband's confidence had dipped so low as to resort to the false claim.

. "What happened, are you feeling okay? You're not looking too well," Mayank asked, turning his attention to her.

"Yeah, I'm okay. Just a minor headache." She knew she had been uncharacteristically mellowed and conveniently attributed it to the headache that had been her companion in the last few years.

Mayank was beginning to realize that it was again a case of bad timing and that the dinner was indeed happening at the wrong time. Sunken faces, after all, did not make for great company. It looked so obvious that Revathi must have struggled a lot to get Pranav for the dinner. But why did she? Mayank wondered. Perhaps she too had feelings for him that she could never confess.

"By the way, Mayank, did you have your BP checked again?" Revathi enquired out of concern.

"Yes, I did. It was slightly high but within control." Then, almost in the same vein, Mayank went on, "I tell you what, Revathi you always tend to overwork yourself. I feel you should learn to relax a bit. I hope that swine, Prabhakar, is not troubling you much with his politics these days."

"No, no, poor thing, he has just recovered from his lung ailment. Now he doesn't meddle with my affairs."

"But I still suggest that you go ahead and start patronizing this new executive, Ramesh and work towards a situation where Prabhakar gets more and more marginalized."

"I guess, yes."

"And did you get the sanction for your expansion plans down south?"

"Yep."

Pranav looked hassled to see that Mayank was privy to the inner goings-on in Revathi's work, and possibly, her personal life. After all he had to idea of whatever politics that Prabhakar was playing on her; Revathi had never told him.

"Shall we order the food?" Pranav quipped, almost assertively. Mayank realized instantly that the conversation between him and Revathi was alienating Pranav. He was quick to make amends.

"Yeah, sure."

"Here what would you like to have?" Pranav put forth the menu in front of Mayank.

"Well, you decide, sir."

"No, no, it's your birthday. The choice should be all yours."

Mayank, for a moment, wondered why Pranav behaved like he was hosting the dinner.

"Okay, I shall go for Macaroni Diavola…"

Some fifteen minutes later, dinner was served. Revathi still looked low and Mayank overly concerned for her.

"Have you got the telecast dates for your serial?" Mayank turned and asked Pranav.

"Not yet. First the pilot needs to get approved."

"I hope they start off soon. It will take a lot of pressure off Revathi."

When Pranav heard this, he had just put a spoon of Pesto Rice inside his mouth. He almost felt choked by the shock of the words. *Oh, so this nerd thinks that Revathi's problems have been caused by me*, he thought, bafflement apparent on his countenance. The absurdity of the statement couldn't escape Revathi either. In a very unsuspecting way, "the confused kid" was beginning to act with the authority that he did not qualify for. Revathi was getting to be aware of the problem that Pranav had forewarned her of. Just that Mayank played his part so innocently that she was left wondering if he was really that innocent or whether he was now employing such statements selectively and testing the waters, as Pranav wanted to make her believe.

"Why don't you take some more rice?" Mayank turned to Revathi.

"Don't worry, I will."

Soon enough, Mayank got a call from Rewa in Delhi. Mayank was cryptic and ended the conversation by telling her that he'll call her back. From the cacophonous sounds of Rewa's voice that was audible to Revathi and Pranav, it could be deciphered that she was pretty excited speaking to her beau.

"So when exactly are you getting married?" Pranav asked, almost out of the blue.

"Well the date has not been decided."

"Looks like you're not happy with the match? Is it so?"

Pranav's sharp query surprised both Mayank and Revathi. Perhaps it was his turn to get back at Mayank. Pranav was really far from being close with Mayank to have asked a personal question like that. Mayank really did not know what to say; Revathi tried being the trouble shooter.

"Pranav, everybody has apprehensions in an arranged marriage. It's only natural. I'm sure Mayank can handle the situation."

Pranav shot back, "Of course, he can. But doesn't he realize that you can handle your problems?"

"What?" Revathi was clearly taken aback by Pranav's tenor.

"Why else does he have to guide you on how you must deal with your colleagues? For that matter why the hell does he have to behave as if your problems are because of me?" Pranav burst out. His face could not hide the deep anguish he felt inside.

This sudden burst sent shock waves in both Revathi and Mayank. Revathi knew that her husband was not feeling positive about their relationship but she had no idea of the level of angst that had stirred up inside him. She was left absolutely speechless, not knowing how to react. The remaining few minutes of the dinner passed off in abject silence. The mood had been spolit beyond repair. And then Pranav ordered for the bill.

When the bill was brought, Pranav took it upon himself. Mayank was surprised to see this. He pulled the bill towards him.

"Wait, I'll pay."

"Oh, come on, give it to me." Pranav pulled the bill back.

Mayank was surprised at this unprovoked tug of war.

"Look, I respect your seniority but this is my treat and I shall pay for it," Mayank asserted.

"What is this, Revathi? Didn't you tell him that we were treating him out?" Pranav protested.

"What?" Mayank couldn't believe it. "Look that's not possible. I really don't know you too well to accept a treat from you on my birthday. The call was mine and I shall pay the bill, that's it."

"Mayank, listen to me," Revathi tried pacifying.

"Come on, Revathi, how is it possible? And why didn't you tell me about this?"

Even when the argument was on, Pranav took out his credit card and gave it the waiter. Mayank retorted by immediately taking out his credit card and giving it to the waiter. He asked the waiter to give Pranav's credit card back to him. Pranav on the other hand repeatedly exhorted the waiter to use his credit card. The waiter looked thoroughly perplexed till Mayank got up angrily, took Pranav's credit card from the waiter, put it in front of Pranav and asked the waiter to go. The waiter looked quite amused at the end of this funny skirmish.

As they waited for the waiter to return, immense awkwardness had by then crept into the situation. The dinner had by no means been half as homely or comforting as Mayank had perhaps hoped it would be. He was already realizing the folly of not having had it with Vishal and Anil, instead.

"Revathi, you should have made things clear. I really don't like this insult," complained Pranav.

Mayank hit back. "What's the insult in this? I mean, I can't imagine myself being forcibly treated by someone else on my birthday."

"Look, Mayank, you must realize that Pranav is much older to you and it doesn't look nice for him to be treated by someone so young," Revathi tried reasoning out, even though she herself didn't sound too confident about the reasoning.

"Maybe, I'd have accepted your point, but point is I hardly know him to accept a treat from him," Mayank retorted.

"Oh, God! Can we please put this aside now? It's my fault and I'm sorry that I somehow tried making things work. But I have realized now that its pointless even trying to bring you both together." Revathi lamented.

Pranav just got up abruptly.

"Yes, it is pointless. Look, Revathi you may treat him like a confused kid. But neither is he confused nor a kid. It will be good for him if he realizes that he's just another friend of yours. He should not try and behave like a husband." Having said, he walked off in a huff.

Revathi had never seen her husband so shaken. Pranav's words resonated in her ears, as though they had been hammered in. She rushed behind him, realizing that a long night of anguish lay ahead.

That night Revathi and Pranav probably had their worst skirmish in a decade. Pranav launched a virulent attack on her. He even accused Revathi of actually having taken a fancy for the younger Mayank and only pretending in front of him that their relationship was purely platonic.

"Why else would you land up in his place and then even go with him to inspect a new flat? Why would you want me to attend his dinner when you could have met him over coffee?" Pranav roared.

And Revathi had no answer. It was a fact she could not escape that she had indeed been too soft on Mayank. She never really found out why.

"It's about time, Revathi, you understand you are becoming a puppet in the hands of this pervert, unless he has begun to give you a kick that I don't," he roared. "Why else would you allow such interference in your personal matters?"

Revathi was stunned. The shock of aspersions being cast on her character made her numb.

'Was she indeed attracted to this young guy- something she herself wasn't aware of?' she wondered.

Pranav went on at his ruthless best.

"Look, I've been involved with a lot of women in my youth to know that such a relationship always has sexual undercurrents. The only reason a young man goes after an older woman is to get pleasure without commitment. It suits him fine but it will destroy you."

Revathi was blown apart by the intensity of his accusation. She had always trusted her husband's judgment. True, that in the last few months, he had perhaps gone through the worst phase of his career. But that it should have affected his judgment to such an extent that he would be grossly incorrect was a little hard to believe. At the same time, Revathi realized that it needed two hands to clap; she had perhaps unknowingly taken some concessions in the relationship, which could have made her lose her objectivity. Relationships, after all are extremely complicated.

That night Revathi could not sleep. She, in fact, wept all night. A problem of this magnitude that had accusations galore was unprecedented in their marriage.

12

Get Set Gay – Part 2

Anil was released from jail after spending a night there; the police had managed to crack the case. Akash had been murdered by his jilted gay partner.

Anil and Rupali's life saw a marked improvement after the fiasco. Anil eventually confided everything in Rupali about his escapade that night, and was surprised by the empathy he got from Rupali. The couple was now beginning to learn to accept each other with the other's baggage. And, Rupali was now keen to be a mother.

It was the day before the Ganapati festival was supposed to start. The Ganapati festivities, being innately imbued in the culture of the city; the residents, irrespective of the different regions of their origin, celebrated the festival with rare, infectious bonhomie. It was one of those occasions where the spirit of the "Mumbaikar" stood out and all residents seemed united. The city bore a festive ambience and people's conversations unfailingly carried a mention of their preparations for the festival. Anil and Rupali had also planned to do a small Puja in their house. Rupali was supposed to return home early that evening so that both husband and wife could venture out together to get the Ganapati home.

Anil accompanied his boss, Ramamurthy for a meeting that day to the JW Marriot Hotel. They were to negotiate a deal with an Indonesian magnate who was in the city and who wanted to invest in the website. Once the meeting was through, Ramamurthy held on to the Indonesian honcho for some more time to discuss matters that they did not want Anil to be privy to. Anil therefore came out to the lounge and waited for his boss to get through. While sitting in the lounge, Anil bumped into a familiar face. Both looked at each other for a few moments before they broke into ruptures of laughter and hugged. It was Govind, once a good friend of Anil's from his college days; they had not been in touch lately. Govind used to be the roommate of a very close friend of Anil in college, Mahesh.

"Hey, you've put on so much, weight, Govind."

"Well, that's the disadvantage of working in a five star hotel's restaurant."

"What? Do you work here?"

Govind informed that he was the restaurant manager in the hotel. The two soon got down to exchanging notes on their respective progress in life and also recalled incidents from the college days.

After initial bonhomie, both got down to talking serious stuff. Govind informed that he was getting married in the next couple of months. Anil, for his part preferred not to speak much about his marriage. Govind did not probe either, but sensing Anil's hurt, couldn't refrain himself from finally making a comment.

"Yaar, Anil, I'm really sorry about Rupali."

The words hit Anil with the most unexpected jolt.

"Sorry? For what?"

"Well, I believe you are separated."

Anil was shocked as he had no clue as to why Govind said this.

"No. Why do you say that?"

"Well, if you're not, there's nothing like it. But I'm sorry that was the impression I got from Mahesh when I told him about the restaurant scene..."

Anil, by now looked completely baffled. He had no idea about what Govind spoke. Govind's half hearted exposition, presumably out of his presumption that Anil knew the rest, only added to the chilling tension that Anil was feeling now.

"Will you please tell me what are you talking? I mean which restaurant scene?"

"You don't know anything?"

Govind informed Anil about having spotted Rupali with Manish at his restaurant last month. They sat like a couple on the corner table and later went out together. This piece of information virtually blew Anil into pieces. He asked Govind if it was possible to find out for him the date when this happened. Govind promised to check the records and let him know by evening as he remembered clearly that Manish had made the payment by a credit card.

About an hour later, Anil returned to office along with Ramamurthy. Ramamurthy instructed him to draft a proposal that was to be sent to the Indonesian magnate that evening itself. Anil however was distracted. He remained in a state of virtual paralytic dysfunction that day. Such indeed was the jolt caused by Govind's news. He even put his mobile on the silent mode and made sure he was not disturbed from any source. Anil saw Rupali's number flashing on his cell twice that afternoon but ignored it.

He knew she must have been calling to find out what time they would meet and go to the market together. He was least bothered. He later found an SMS from her: *Hi! Get some fruits and an agarbattii pack on your way home.*

That evening Govind called up Anil and confirmed Anil's worst fears. Rupali and Manish had indeed gone for dinner on night of August 11 – the night he had his gay escapade. Anil knew now that Rupali's Pune trip was a sham. She had probably taken the day off to be with her ex-lover and paramour. Anil felt all his emotions for her dying with this news.

Anil returned home that night only to find Rupali waiting for him.

"Where were you Anil? I called you twice but you didn't respond. In fact, I've placed an order for the Ganapati idol."

Rupali realized that all was perhaps not well. "What happened, did the meeting go off well?"

Anil did not say anything. He just drank a few glasses of water. Rupali realized that in his preoccupation Anil had forgotten to get home the fruits and agarbattis.

"Don't worry, you just take a shower and get ready for dinner. I'll go and buy the remaining stuff."

That night, dinner was a pretty solemn affair. Anil spoke almost monosyllabically and when Rupali tried to probe if something was amiss, he remained rather curt and evasive. Anil's withdrawn behavior continued when the couple went to bed. Rupali found it a little unprovoked, especially since communication between them had been improving lately. She therefore, decided to reverse positions for once. She tried enticing Anil into sex and the result was a blast. Anil slapped her hard. His eyes were consumed with hatred.

"You bitch! You were warming Manish's bed at the Marriot that night when you told me you went to Pune?"

Rupali was stunned by the suddenness of Anil's eruption.

"Look, Anil…"

Anil slapped her hard again.

"I've sacrificed so much for you, Rupali. I've almost been living on your terms all these years. And this is what I get from you in return? You are so bloody disgusting. Shameless! I hate you, you whore."

Anil stormed out of the room and banged the door upon her. That night, Anil couldn't sleep. He lay on the sofa, hurt and anguished. He was feeling terribly cheated by the one girl he loved. The feelings of hurt and anguish were simultaneously leading to a more intense emotion— a feeling of violent hatred. Yes, he now despised her for sure. Anil felt very strongly that he would divorce his wife as soon as possible. After a while, he tried drawing solace in an old whisky bottle that he had kept in reserve. He did hear the sound of Rupali sobbing inside but was least bothered. He drank till the wee hours of the morning. At maybe six in the morning, he finally fell asleep, but only for a couple of hours. At eight, he was woken up by the constant ringing of the doorbell. He wondered in anger why Rupali couldn't do so much as to open the door.

Anil opened the door to find a person standing with the Ganapati Idol. He informed that 'madam' had ordered for it. Anil took the Idol in, almost dispassionately. Anil wondered where Rupali was. *Would she still be shameless enough to expect that they perform the puja together,* he wondered.

Anil avoided even thinking about her and decided to get on instead with his daily chores. A few minutes later, he heard her cell phone ring. The sound was obviously coming from inside the room. It kept ringing for a while but the call wasn't taken. A few moments later, the cell phone rang again; and again it wasn't taken. Anil got a bit alarmed by this. He decided to at least check if she was in the room.

He opened the door to get the shock of his life. Rupali lay unconscious even as a trace of saliva could be seen on her face. She had apparently consumed a whole bottle of sleeping pills. Just beside her left palm was a letter that she had written to explain her action. It was a long letter that Anil was just not interested in reading at that point. Anil rushed her to the hospital, aided by a neighbor.

Even as Rupali was operated upon, the hospital wore a relatively deserted look. Faint echoes of *Ganapati Bappa Maurya* could be heard off and on in the vicinity. Anil stood in one corner on the verandah biting his nail and desperately hoping that Rupali would be saved. He remembered having squeezed the letter that he found on Rupali's bed into his trouser pocket. He took it out and read it, trepidation of the consequences of her confessions, writ large on her face. The letter went thus:

Anil,

In life there are no facts, only interpretations. I feel guilty of not having given you the love and attention that I could always sense you expected from me. I always wanted to but I guess I was a weak character who could never get out of living in the past.

Today, somehow I feel there is no point continuing to live in this manner. But I do wish to tell you the truth about the night of August 11.

I had been to Pune as planned. My work got over early and I returned to office at about 9pm to leave behind some important documents. When I reached office I got the shock of my life to find Manish waiting for me. Manish looked disturbed and shaken. He wanted to talk to me and virtually cajoled me to have dinner with him. Since he was staying at the J W Marriot, we had dinner there. During dinner, he told me all about his turbulent life. He had married a girl in the States. Unfortunately his wife died within months in an accident for which his in-laws started blaming him. Subsequently Manish lost his job. Now he wanted to come back to India and start afresh. He stunned me by saying that he wanted to marry me. When I protested against his audacity, he told me that my whole friend circle believed that I was not happy with you. I felt ashamed that day because it came as a slur on my character, on my being. After that meeting with Manish, for the first time, I felt that I had failed as a wife. And it was so obvious that everybody seemed to know.

Yet, my conscience wanted me to go in for correction rather than escape. In the emotional quagmire that I found myself trapped in that night, I was really feeling awkward to come in front of you. I was actually feeling petty.

I called up my childhood friend, Mona and spent that whole night talking with her in her Vkhroli flct. I came back in the morning, determined to tell you the truth about the previous night and start afresh. Bu tinstead I saw policemen waiting to arrest you and we were trapped in a new set of problems.... Subsequently I cut off all channels of communication with Manish and even did not take his calls.

Today when you called me a whore, I didn't feel aggrieved somehow. I realized that if the person who has loved me the

*most was saying that to me, I had gone terribly wrong somewhere.
Perhaps, my case was even beyond redemption.*

I'm ending my life because I am feeling ashamed of myself.

Rupali

Anil squirmed on the wooden bench when he read this. He knew he was a loser. He felt a strange sinking feeling engulf him completely. Somehow, he more or less conditioned himself to face the doctor, who he thought would come out of the Operation Theatre and apologize to him for not being able to save Rupali. He didn't know exactly why such a stark thought descended upon him. Perhaps he had stopped expecting positive happenings in life anymore.

A few minutes later, the bearded middle age doctor came out of the Operation Theatre and informed, to Anil's astonishment, that Rupali had been saved and was even partially conscious. Anil couldn't believe it and verified a second time if the doctor was talking about the lady in the late twenties who had consumed sleeping pills. And when the doctor confirmed, his joy knew no bounds.

A few moments later, Anil stepped into the room where Rupali was kept. Rupali was awake, though unimaginably frail. Anil looked guilty and shaken. He had that letter in one hand, which he then tore into pieces. There was awkwardness in his steps. Rupali's expression was rather blank. She knew she had done her part of the talking. Now it was Anil's turn. Anil stood beside her bed and looked into her eyes. It was as if a whole gamut of emotions had converged into this one moment. He bent and knelt on the floor and then gave her a kiss on her forehead. When he looked into Rupali's eyes, he couldn't hold his emotions back. He broke down. Rupali felt just as miserable seeing her husband cry like this. She had seen him like this only once before. That was when Anil had lost his mother. Rupali could never have forgotten the sight of Anil holding on to his mother's dead body and crying inconsolably. Then he had lost his mother, now it was the shock of nearly losing the only woman in his life. Within moments, she was crying as helplessly as her husband. An onlooker would perhaps have got the impression that both were competing on the quantity of tears each could shed. They hugged each other finally and it looked as if their combined tears had washed away all the dirt from their lives.

Later that evening, when Anil was heading home, he came across a small Ganapati Idol that had been installed inside the hospital campus near the gate. He stopped by to say a prayer. After all, it was divine intervention that had saved Rupali. He prayed like a purged disciple and ended up reciting the whole Ganesh Chaturthi that his mother had made him learn in his younger days. He remained in meditation for sometime till he was brought out of it finally by the sound of the *aarti*. He looked unencumbered when he came out of meditation, though.

An onlooker, who watched his behavior, was impressed that Anil had spent nearly an hour in silent meditation.

13

Confessions of a Dangerous Mind

Hazaron khwaaishein aisi ki har khwaaish pe dum nikle,
Bahut nikle mere armaan, lekin phir bhi kam nikle

— Ghalib

A stage had come when in Revathi's words, "too much water had flown under the bridge." When Revathi actually said this, Mayank could not make out which bridge she was talking about. At times he wondered if this insurmountable bridge was her husband. After all, Pranav did come across as being as unresponsive as a non-living entity.

Twelve days had gone by and Mayank had not spoken with Revathi even once. He did send a couple of SMSs though, about two days ago. The first was a feel good message that read- *One day love and friendship met. Love asked, "Why do you exist if I already exist?" Friendship replied, "To put a smile where you leave tears."* Mayank was obviously testing waters when he sent that, intending to find out how Revathi would react. In a metaphorical way, he was perhaps also trying to clarify that the recent incidents notwithstanding, their relationship was still friendship and not love, as her husband might have had her believe. In a very subtle way, he was perhaps also trying to gain a moral high ground over Pranav, who was by now seeming more and more cynical. Mayank, however, knew better than anybody else that he was simply beating around the bush.

In all previous occasions when he had sent a feel good message like that, Revathi had responded with a benevolent, "Thanks, God Bless You." This time however, there was no response. By evening he had sent another SMS that read a cryptic, yet concerned "How are you?" It again did not get him any response. It hurt Mayank. After all, he had got used to being responded by her with unfailing promptness. In this chaotic frame of mind, Mayank was finding it difficult to concentrate on work.

Vishal, who was witness to Mayank's anguish tried to talk him out of the mess. For a change, Vishal resorted to poetry and used the lyrics of an old Hindi film song to drive home his point:

"Taruf (feelings) rog ho jaye to usko bhulna behtar,
Taluk (relationship) bojh ban jaye to usko todana achchha…
Woh afasana jise anjam tak lana na ho mumkin,
Usse ek khubsoorat mod dekar chhodana achcha"

Mayank liked the poetry but was not sure if he could let go of the relationship just like that.

"But what do you get out of it?" Anil asked him bluntly.

Mayank was stumped by the directness of the question. Mayank hoped that Anil would himself answer the question, rather than bring it to a state where Mayank would have to make an embarrassing statement.

"Probably she doesn't in the least see you the way you want her to. She just considers you a friend," Anil reasoned.

Mayank at this point hit back.

"Hey look. We all have enough female friends to know that

this is not just friendship. She wants to be with me and talk to me as much as I do. When I'm hurt, I know it hurts her as well. Trust me, it's only her responsibilities of being wife and mother that prevent her from coming out in the open and accepting her feelings."

"Look, Mayank, you are fooling yourself. Why don't you talk about this with her and you'll know the truth."

For once, Anil seemed to have spoken with unprecedented clarity and surprisingly, he was not far off target. His words reminded Mayank about something Revathi herself had told him a few days back.

"Look, it's very easy to lose objectivity and get carried away in the kind of equations that we share. Therefore, if my husband feels that there is something wrong about it, I respect his judgment; it always needs a third person to tell you when you are going overboard," Revathi had said. Mayank was naturally a little upset when she said that; he would have been happier if she did not mind going overboard. Nonetheless, Revathi was accepting that she too may have gone overboard.

Anil added, "Besides, you better get this clear that your constant need to meet her has to do with an 'unachieved agenda' that you have with her."

The last sentence of Anil almost struck Mayank like lightning. The 'unachieved agenda' that Anil spoke of, was obviously a physical intercourse. Was it really that, which had made him so restless? Mayank probed into his mind. For almost half an hour thereafter, he kept wondering if his body language and behavior had become so obviously indicative of his mental state that even a relatively less intelligent person like Anil could pass judgments on him. And was it really that, he kept thinking.

Mayank actually had two very disparate thought processes on in his mind that kept contradicting each other. On the one hand perhaps Anil was correct in his own way. A physical relationship was obviously a very natural culmination to the mental and emotional compatibility that Mayank and Revathi shared. But the second thought was far too frightening. It revolved around the classic friend-lover dilemma. If he ever dared to even drop a hint to Revathi that he was interested in a physical relationship with her, he stood the risk of losing her as friend forever. And Mayank never ever would have wanted that to happen; such was the support that talking to Revathi gave him. Their conversations were so stimulating that they amounted to 'surrogate sex', in any case, he felt.

The constant thought of Revathi had made Mayank that much more desperate to hear her voice once again. Moreover, there was a juvenile spurt in him that made him feel he should confess to Revathi that he had indeed felt drawn to her; that perhaps he loved her. He even visualized himself saying that to Revathi subconsciously. However, that very moment, he dreaded her reaction and wondered why on earth, did he want to commit hara-kiri. The quest for experience and adventure, however, kept spurring him on to do it. Mayank reasoned out to himself that if their relationship had to end, it was only apt that it ended with the most honest confession he could ever make.

Mayank, even though, he was dying to speak to Revathi, somehow prevented himself from calling her up, lest that should lead to another ugly scene at her house. He instead mulled hard and thought of a way she could be made to call him back. A thought, a rather weird one at that, occurred to him and without thinking twice, he instantly sent an SMS. It read: "I'm going to London for a while. Won't you call and wish me luck?"

A recurring attack of migraine had kept Revathi at home that day. When she got this message, Pranav was in the same room.

"What happened? Whose message is it that you look so tense?" enquired Pranav.

"Mayank's. He has written he is going abroad."

Pranav took the cell-phone and read it.

"Good that he's gonna be away. Call him. He wants you to wish him luck," Pranav sounded indifferent, yet well intentioned.

Revathi dialed Mayank's number. When her fingers pressed the phone buttons, she virtually trembled. Hurt, after all, had come to be an inescapable element in their relationship of late.

"Hi, Mayank, my best wishes are always with you. When are you leaving?"

"Well, I would have, if you hadn't called." Mayank sounded so naturally callous as ever.

"What?"

"Yes, actually, I'm really sorry but I just wanted to hear your voice, since I was worried…"

"You mean that thing about your going to London was a lie."

Mayank fumbled for an answer and Revathi became furious.

"Are you mad? Do you understand that I'm not your bosom buddy with whom you can play all these games…?" Revathi roared uncharacteristically.

"But Revathi, if I had called you, I didn't know whether you would speak or not."

"Stop it, Mayank. Your behavior has left me faceless in front of my husband and now let me tell you that it's affecting my family. So, please don't ever call me again." Revathi banged the phone. Pranav was witness to the whole incident but chose not to add to the tension. He knew that Mayank's stupid behavior was a vindication of the point he was trying to make.

For Mayank, Revathi's words were devastating. He was so infuriated that be banged his cell phone in disgust. Luckily the old Nokia 3315 model was sturdy enough to withstand the impact.

That night, when Pranav lay with Revathi on the bed, he found her unusually shaken. While on the one hand, Revathi's strong sense of commitment towards her husband stood out like always, there was something that was bothering her and which kept her gloomy. He realized that she was perhaps upset at the way she had behaved with Mayank. Or possibly being a genuinely good human, it was her concern for Mayank. After all, to be a good wife, she had all of a sudden become insensitive to a good friend. That Mayank was quietly suffering must have hurt Revathi for sure, he thought. Strangely enough, the situation didn't anger Pranav today. Instead, he empathized with her. The introspective soul that Pranav tended to be at times, he realized at this point that talking themselves out of the difficult situation made better sense.

"Are you alright?"

"Yes."

Pranav knew she wasn't.

"What do I do Pranav? You were right. Somewhere I have erred. I have allowed things to drift to this level," conceded Revathi.

"Good you realize this. The fault is mine too. I do understand that coping with my professional uncertainties hasn't been easy on you. You needed friends who you could talk too. Your bad luck, you got this obsessive lover. Such are the ironies of life I guess."

"But how do I come out of it?"

Pranav thought for a moment.

"Meet Mayank once."

Revathi just looked in surprise wanting him to say more.

"Yes, I feel, you must meet him one last time and make him understand his folly. I guess it must be hard on Mayank to suddenly be cut off from you. After all, I have seen his dependence on you. A one to one meeting will perhaps help you end contact on a more amiable and happy note. Or else these complexities will never get sorted. "

Revathi was glad to see this empathizing side of Pranav at this difficult moment. It was basically Pranav's ability to see reason in the other person that had drawn her to him in the early years. Though this quality showed up only occasionally in recent years, but when it did, it always came as a rock solid reassurance for Revathi.

That night Mayank, too, did a lot of introspection. He finally concluded that he must treat Revathi as a closed chapter, perhaps the most confusing one in his life. The words and suggestions of Anil and Vishal kept coming back into his mind and he realized that he had perhaps willingly allowed objectivity to go for a toss.

The next morning Mayank sauntered into the office some half an hour late. His countenance reflected that he was short on sleep. Nonetheless, there was an air of optimism in his stride. The optimism stemmed from the knowledge that he was out of whatever messy bond that Revathi and he shared. He surmised that most disappointments resulted due to expectations and now that he didn't have any expectations from Revathi, he was entitled not to be disappointed. Mayank had, in fact made an impromptu call to Rewa on his way to office and felt a positive energy radiate in him from the effect of it.

Mayank got down to work and started sorting out the mess

that his incoherence in the last few days had landed him in. He got a call then and was quite surprised to see that the caller was Revathi.

"Hi Mayank, how are you?" Revathi sounded as warm and friendly as he had normally known her to be.

"I'm okay."

"Mayank, can we meet today? I want to talk to you."

"Well, yes. Mocha, in the evening?"

Mayank did not know what spurred him on to instantaneously jump at the opportunity of a meeting; that too when he just looked like having conditioned himself into a different mindset prior to getting the call. Mayank realized that he was perhaps still too irresolute in the case of Revathi. Or that perhaps deep in his heart of hearts he was dying to meet her, no matter what he tried to make himself believe.

There was nearly a quarter of a day to go for meeting time, but he was already caught in major quandary. *What does Revathi want to talk to me about now after all that's happened? After all, only yesterday, she was so furious and said she never wanted to speak to me again. Does she, for a change, want to take me into confidence on something her husband needs to be kept out of?* Mayank kept thinking about myriad possibilities. One thing which he felt convinced about was that he did mean something to her and that he did affect her emotionally. This, he thought was a sure enough sign that Revathi was equally inclined to the relationship. After all, Anil would always tell him that his feelings were one sided. Mayank now felt doubly sure they weren't that unilateral.

Till the time Mayank reached Mocha, he was not able to concentrate on work at all. His quandary remained unsorted still; he had absolutely no idea of what could transpire at the meeting.

Finally just before meeting time, gusty winds lashed the city – a precursor perhaps of a burst of the receding monsoons. And the windy freshness surely eased to some extent the strain that both Mayank and Revathi felt. Mayank wondered how the rains got to know about all their meetings. Mayank arrived in Vishal's borrowed car. Revathi arrived in her chauffeur driven one.

When Mayank and Revathi sat face to face, both realized that there was something unusual about this meeting compared with their previous meetings. On previous occasions, Revathi would be all chilled out and talk to Mayank like she would with a kid. However, this time around, she was consciously restrained. It was as if she was trying hard to adhere to a protocol. It also made Mayank feel that he was suddenly an adult and an equal in front of her.

Mayank tried easing the tension by enquiring about her chauffeur and maid problems. Revathi however was in no mood to play ball. Mayank knew this meeting had something really dramatic in store. He gulped half a glass of water that was laid in front of him, as though the water would wash away his nervousness.

Without wasting time, Revathi got down to talking business.

"Actually, the reason I called you here is to make you understand why we need to give each other a break."

"Break?"

"Look, I understand my husband lost his cool on your birthday but perhaps for the first time I also failed to realize that a lot of unpleasant feelings were bottling up within him…"

Mayank cut her short and sounded almost defiant. "I don't understand this. You expect tons of maturity from me, but your husband who is thirteen years elder to me will continue behaving like a traffic constable."

'What? What did you say?"

"I mean what he is doing is policing. Why can't he trust his wife? What have we done?"

"Look, Mayank, let me clarify this once and for all. It's not that he doesn't trust me. It's a matter of another man gaining so much unnecessary importance in my life. And mind you, if you put yourself in his position, you will realize he has a point."

Mayank did not know what to say and slipped into defense. "But a rational person would still not behave that way."

"A rational person may not, but a protective husband surely will."

Revathi looked hassled by now. In front of her were two glasses of water, one full and the other half full.

"Which one of this is yours?" she asked irritated.

Mayank was too done in with the situation to react immediately. Revathi took the glass that was half full. Mayank just looked in surprise- Revathi was indeed an unusual being. She had retained all her niceties even in this turbulent moment.

"So, is that your final word?" asked Mayank.

"Look, Mayank I'm not here to argue. I'm fond of you and would like to be that way. But I really cannot take the stress that this relationship is causing me. You may not like the way my husband behaved but he is my husband and has certain rights over me which you don't."

A few moments later, tension still prevailed. Mayank sipped his ice tea and looked pensive. Revathi too sipped her tea but she did it with some urgency as though she wanted to just complete it and go. Never would she have imagined that in just about three and a half months from the time she first met Mayank, she would have to contend with an interaction of this unusual sort.

"Mayank, I hope you will think about what I've said with an open mind. Try and understand my position. Is there anything you want to say?"

Mayank took a long pause before nodding.

"Shoot."

"Are you really happy with Pranav?"

Revathi was shocked by the directness with which he said these inflammable words.

"Why do you ask me this question?"

Mayank took another long pause. All along his expression couldn't mask the risk factor that was weighing on his mind. He spoke finally trying to sound as confident as he looked.

"Because....because I love you."

Revathi was zapped to hear this and had no idea of how to react. She was angry, shocked, empathizing, all at once. And when she spoke, her speech and her expression bore mutual dichotomy.

"Are you crazy? Have you gone mad? Do you understand what you are saying?"

"Yes. That's the most honest sentence I have ever said to you."

Revathi was just too numb for any definite reaction. She could sense the floor beneath her feet sink with the impact of what Mayank had said. She was still not sure whether she was imagining the situation or whether it had actually happened. Seeing her shock, Mayank, who still seemed pretty convinced, perhaps gradually began to realize the blasphemy he had committed.

"Look, our relationship is destined. Your presence is written on the palm of my hand," Mayank said, pointing out the two lines on the upper right end of his right palm. He looked both desperate and helpless.

Revathi couldn't believe it. She remembered telling Mayank about those lines.

"Look Revathi, don't get me wrong. You only told me that this upper line is just an affair and trust me it was Shweta. The bottom one that leads to marriage is actually you. Trust me, this is you."

Revathi was trembling by the repeated shocks inflicted by Mayank's pronouncements. Mayank was equally nervous, yet determined. He hadn't planned to say all that he did. Perhaps he realized he wouldn't get another opportunity.

This was the inevitability that Revathi had feared lately. She however hadn't in the remotest manner anticipated that it would hit her all of a sudden and catch her unawares.

"Revathi what are you thinking? I want an answer from you," Mayank re-inforced himself.

"About what?"

"Look into my eyes. You too love me."

"Are you crazy?'

"We both are. If you're not, ask yourself why you enjoy talking to me when your husband wants to make love to you? Why do you call me and come over to my place when we weren't talking? Why do you share all your daily problems with me like you would with a life partner? Come on give me answers." A defiant Mayank charged.

Revathi was stunned. She'd never imagined being grilled in this manner, that too by Mayank.

"Look Revathi you talk about my indulgence and my body language. But haven't you always said that you need two hands to clap? Haven't you ever realized that I am attracted to you? I'm sure you have. And yet, I have seen how free and comfortable you have felt in my company. Why? Come on, tell me."

Mayank's decibel levels were high enough to invite attention of people around. Revathi was embarrassed and called for the waiter.

"Mayank, I have to go."

Revathi wanted to pay but Mayank stopped her. Mayank, empowered by his gutsy confessions, was determined to pool in a bigger share.

"From now it's got to be fifty-fifty. I'm no longer your one-third partner," Mayank asserted, his demeanor more authoritative than child-like.

Revathi just looked too tired to argue with him over what appeared a very trivial matter now. She seemed to be in a pressing hurry to retreat. She got up to leave. Mayank just held her hand, raising the shock value to unprecedented levels

"Revathi you can't go like this. You still haven't answered me."

Revathi pulled her hand away.

"I don't owe you any answers. Is that clear?"

Revathi left abruptly. But barely had she reached the exit that she realized it was raining fairly heavily. Moreover, her chauffeur whom she had sent off to get the car lights repaired, hadn't arrived yet. Revathi waited at the exit hoping her chauffeur would arrive with the car. However, he didn't and the rains only got heavier. In fact, it was the kind of heavy rainfall that showed up only once or twice in the season. Even the cell phone signals had gone off. Mayank finally persuaded her to come in his car. In the sheer chaos that prevailed all around, Revathi did not see a better option. She knew the drive back home was not going to be easy, in any case.

As they drove back, Mayank at the wheel, Revathi beside him, shock got the better of her. While Mayank tried hard to see through the fading visibility, Revathi recollected her ten odd meetings with him that had unsuspectingly led her to a weird situation where she had this young guy propose to her. She tried to gather herself. Strangely enough, she was hassled and torn no doubt, but she did not hate Mayank for this; and she wondered why. Revathi wondered what she would tell Pranav about her meeting. After all, she had met Mayank this time around on Pranav's instruction. She wondered for a moment if she could hide the truth about what Mayank had said to her from Panav. After all, her husband too might not be telling her all that he and Sonal spoke. But this thought was only momentary and frivolous. True to her character, Revathi decided that she will tell all to her husband the way it happened.

However barely had they reached the Juhu circle, when they found the roads flooded with knee deep water. Traffic was completely jammed. In fact, shockingly enough, a few cars were left stranded without anyone in it – an ominous indicator of how violent the rains must have been. Further up towards Andheri and Lokhandwala, the water levels must have been higher because there was absolutely no movement of traffic from there on. Both Revathi and Mayank tried calling friends and acquaintances but to no avail. The mobile services were totally jammed. And in this quagmire, Revathi and Mayank saw the worst- some distance away, a human corpse floated in the water. Revathi almost puked.

A couple of hours later, Revathi and Mayank were still stranded at the same place. They knew that they would probably have to spend the whole night in much the same manner. Even the street lights were off. They realized that if they were to walk home, they might have to wade through more corpses. Staying inside the car, though suffocating for reasons concerning both the weather and their personal equations was still a safer option. It was still raining continuously, though not as ferociously. Mayank blabbered a bit about these conditions; Revathi was by and large silent.

It was only around midnight that they broke the ice and started chatting normally. Unable to bear nature's call, Mayank had already gone on the back seat and peed once in an empty can, meant to stock petrol. They knew they would have to kill another few hours or so before they could think of treading homewards. Revathi however made Mayank promise that he would not talk anything about their relationship. She was game to talking anything else.

Till morning thereafter, Revathi spoke largely about issues concerning emancipation of women. Mayank, for his part, spoke about India's flawed foreign policy. They did this for hours to avoid the mention of the issue that had the potential of causing a deluge, far bigger in devastation than the one they were witnessing outside.

14

An Unhappy Family

It was nearly six in the morning and still dark, when Mayank escorted Revathi to her building. Pranav, who had been wandering distraught all across the house, all through the night, saw this from his balcony. He heaved a huge sigh of relief. This was when he hadn't yet registered that the man accompanying her was Mayank. Pranav's relief was overcome with apprehensions in no time. He knew Revathi was supposed to meet the guy. But were they together the whole of this wet night?

Revathi rushed inside in near frenzy only to find that it was pitch dark. There was no electricity. She checked out instantly if her daughter and husband were alright. Her husband was; her daughter wasn't. Ria who was at a friend's place in the adjoining building when the deluge occurred and had had to wade through chest deep water to reach home, appeared terribly shaken. She was already running temperature.

Revathi recounted the details of her night of horror to her husband. Pranav seemed just numb. Revathi gathered the cause, but just couldn't get herself to talk on the issue any further, given the chaos that prevailed.

A couple of hours later, after settling things somewhat, Pranav and Revathi sat over the breakfast table. Strangely enough, a rather deafening silence prevailed between the couple. Revathi tried breaking it.

"Gosh! I never thought I would see such an occurrence. Can you believe it, there was a human corpse floating in the streets right at the Juhu circle?"

Pranav heard it out; but remained unusually reticent, almost indifferent. Revathi wondered if he already knew about Mayank having proposed to her and was only putting up a pretence. Incidentally, both Pranav and Revathi were in disarray for their own reasons. Interestingly enough, neither of them knew about the other's reason. Revathi kept wondering how she should tell Pranav about Mayank's behavior. Almost instantly she wondered if at all that needed to be told. But again, not telling it was something she could not do; after all Pranav was privy to every single occurrence in her life, the way she had wanted things to be. Pranav too was preoccupied. The sight of Revathi being dropped home by Mayank, on this rainy day, sure hurt him. There was however another reason for his disappointment. The "pilot" he had shot for Sony, had been rejected. Pranav was informed of this rejection barely a couple of hours before the flooding started the previous day. As such Revathi did not even know about it. And to add to the woes of the couple, was the larger chaos that prevailed all over. There was no electricity. Water was scarcely coming from just one tap connected with an overhead tank. And in the absence of any concrete information, the safety of friends and acquaintances was a cause of worry.

That whole day nothing really happened except waiting for things to get normal. The couple got a few calls from worried outstation relatives. Electricity was finally restored at around 5 in the evening. And no sooner had that happened the couple got an insight into just how devastating the floods had been. Images shot from a helicopter and shown on NDTV made it appear a calamity as huge as the one caused by the *tsunami*.

At around 11 pm, the couple lay in bed, the way they normally did before falling asleep. Pranav surfed through the news channels; Revathi just checked something out on her cell phone diary. Beneath the superficial veil of normalcy was Revathi's hasty determination that she would tell Pranav everything tonight about what Mayank had told her. She prepared the ground for it.

"Pranav, why don't you switch off the television please? It's the same heart wrenching images that they have been showing since evening."

Pranav could sense that she probably wanted to speak to him about something. However, right at this point, her cell rang. It was Mayank.

"Yeah," Revathi responded curtly.

"Revathi, is everything alright? "

"Yes."

"Oh, thank God. I was really worried since you remained in wet clothes for so long."

Pranav knew whose call it was. He increased the volume of the TV. It became so loud that the conspiracy theory couldn't escape Mayank. He nonetheless continued.

"Anyway, Revathi, you must take a Doxycelene tablet. It's very useful in dealing with these situations."

Revathi cut the phone. Mayank was startled by the abrupt ending of the conversation, but gathered it was deliberate. Revathi could sense that Pranav was looking at her rather indignantly. She couldn't blame him either at this point, especially after what she had experienced.

"Pranav, I want to talk to you."

Pranav nearly ignored her. He was watching the images of Kurla submerged completely in chest deep water.

"Pranav, can I have a word with you?" she reiterated.

"Yeah… sure."

Pranav could sense what it would be. For a moment, he wondered if she was ditching him for Mayank. Almost instantly he rubbished the weird idea. He knew for sure, though, that Revathi had never looked so serious.

"What is the matter?"

Just as Revathi was about to speak, Pranav got a call. It was Sonal. Pranav heard her out for a moment before he spoke.

"Yeah, Sonal, I know the losses are going to be huge. In fact, I doubt if we will be able to pay anyone."

Revathi gathered that something was amiss and that it had to do with the 'pilot'.

"Yeah, but who is going to explain to these fucking channel people… that's why I was dead against the idea of shooting a pilot without any contract."

Revathi knew that the pilot had been rejected. She knew it was going to be a far longer night for them than what she had imagined.

An hour later, they were still awake. Revathi was completely absorbed in Pranav's disappointment, so much so that her own dilemmas had been relegated into an unimportant zone.

"What do I do, Revathi? There was a time when nothing seemed to go wrong for me, and now nothing goes right for me." Pranav moaned like a kid, "I'm sure it's the effect of *Rahu*. Oh God, its still three years before the positive effect of *Brahaspat* is going to start on me."

Pranav, of late, had started believing in astrology. He would regularly consult an astrologer in Dadar and religiously pursue his instructions. For Revathi, this looked so strange. She recalled a time when she had a miscarriage a few months into their marriage. A depressed Revathi had blamed it in on the stars, only to be rubbished by her husband. "Are you crazy? In this age, you think these things can be attributed to stars?" Revathi wished she could say the same to Pranav now. His state unfortunately required care more than anything else.

Pranav suddenly remembered that Revathi too had been meaning to chat with him.

"You wanted to tell me something."

Revathi didn't know what to say. She looked unusually tentative, perhaps even shy. Pranav hadn't seen her like this in ages. The last time he remembered seeing her like this was when they had made love for the first time, a few months before getting married. Revathi had actually looked like a meek and obedient disciple, grateful for having imbibed a new lesson. There was perhaps an iota of guilt also on her countenance at that point. After all, that was her first physical indulgence.

Pranav did not know so much about female psychology as to correctly decipher why Revathi looked that way once again. But he gathered that it must have had something to do with her state of mind vis-à-vis two very different men, one rightfully demanding her attention and the other unjustifiably clamoring for it. One flicker of a nightmarish thought had him wonder if Revathi had been proposed by Mayank. But almost instantly he realized the absurdity of it.

"Hey come on, what's the matter? I'm sure Mayank didn't propose to you," Pranav laughed it off as he got up and checked himself in the mirror.

Revathi was calm, just about.

"He did."

Pranav could see his expression changing in a bizarre sort of way in the mirror.

"What? What did Mayank do?"

"He said he's in love with me," Revathi confessed with the honesty of a young kid who had been caught stealing chocolates.

Surprisingly, it was not something that Pranav was entirely unprepared for. And though Revathi coolly went on to explain the context, as also how she had dealt with the situation, for Pranav a point of no return seemed to have come. He just flared up in a cathartic way.

"Look Revathi, you wanted it to happen. You have really brought it upon yourself," he roared, pain and anger laced in his voice in equal measure.

"What are you saying, Pranav?"

"Only the truth. I had warned you so many times against this boy, but you didn't listen. Fact is, whether you accept it or not, you have developed the hots for this young guy. You are as much in love with him as he is with you."

The decimating impact of this last statement virtually turned Revathi's world upside down. This was, not in the least the reaction she would have anticipated from her husband. Pranav, on his part, looked so shaken that he just stormed out.

⁓

As tears flowed down her cheek, Revathi remembered an incident that had taken place nearly five years ago. She was working as an

Account Director with an Advertising Agency at that point. Her boss, Mehta, a charmer in his mid forties, a divorcee and also a family friend had made a pass at her in the most unsuspecting of ways.

Revathi and her boss, Mr. Mehta, were driving down to Cuffe Parade for a presentation to the client. They were almost certain to bag the account. While driving down, they ended up discussing the incident of an aspiring actress who had filed a case of rape against a renowned film director for sexually exploiting her.

While Revathi steadfastly condemned the director, Mehta strangely differed with her.

"Look my friend, to get something, you need to give something. There is no dearth of talent in this overpopulated country. In that case, if you want to surge ahead, you must learn to compromise."

Mehta had said this last sentence tapping her thighs, a gesture Revathi found suggestive and even lewd.

A couple of days later, they got the account. And Mehta asked her out for dinner. Revathi cooked up an alibi to skip the rendezvous. But since Mehta was insistent that 'they needed to move fast on the new account', Revathi relented eventually after taking Pranav's consent.

That night, Mehta had got drunk and crossed the limit.

"You are the most attractive woman I have seen. Just do as I say and see what I do to your career," he kept repeating in a semi inebriated state, tapping her thighs more confidently.

That night Revathi had confided everything in Pranav. Pranav had protected her with kid-gloves, tutoring her on how to handle the situation.

"Just make sure that from tomorrow, you give him a clear indication that you will talk just work with him and nothing else. Be very polite yet very firm."

Revathi, thereafter, adhered to the list of dos and don'ts provided to her by Pranav. Though Mehta retracted and looked almost apologetic there on, she was replaced from the account, for no valid reason. However, with Pranav firmly by her side, a minor professional setback didn't mean a thing to her.

When Revathi confided in Pranav today, she was perhaps seeking the same support and protection.

Pranav instead wanted to be left alone. He spent the whole night on the sofa in the living room. Revathi thought a couple of times of speaking to him and assuaging him. But every time she did this, Pranav's insulting remark about her fetish for Mayank would resonate in her ears. It hurt her lots; it made her feel ashamed. After all, the statement amounted to casting aspersions on her character, a thing she had never imagined her husband would do.

The next morning Pranav left home early and didn't return till late in the night. Revathi called him once out of concern, only to be told cryptically that he was busy and would call her back. Revathi just couldn't concentrate on her work the whole day.

Even at a half past ten in the night, Pranav wasn't home. Revathi knew where he would be. Simultaneous emotions of hurt, betrayal, deceit thronged her mind. Ria kept asking why Dad wasn't home. Revathi finally called Pranav.

"Are you planning to come home or have you shifted permanently?"

Revathi never quite sounded acerbic in normal circumstances. But today, the situation was just far from normal. Pranav too lost his cool.

"Why? Don't you have Mayank for company tonight?" Pranav turned to Sonal, "Sonal, will you please reduce the TV volume?"

For Revathi, hearing the last sentence was like the last straw. How could Pranav, sitting at Sonal's place make such a crude remark on her?

"You are really so cheap and disgusting Pranav." Revathi banged the phone.

Revathi knew it was going to be another long night for her. She kept awake till late. Her eyes must have just succumbed to exhaustion finally when she heard a few loud knocks on the door. She ran and opened it. There was Pranav, standing in an inebriated state, virtually clinging on to Sonal, who stood supporting him. Pranav seemed to be out of his senses.

"Well, Pranav just went overboard with the drink. I thought I'd drop him home," Sonal rendered an explanation, trying hard to overcome her awkwardness.

Pranav for his part took control of himself and walked in, albeit with crooked steps. Soon enough, he hit the bed in sheer oblivion of everything around.

That whole night, Revathi sat out on the sofa. Pranav's caustic admonishment of her on the phone and the sight of him clinging onto Sonal were incidences that seemed irretrievably etched on her psyche. She just hated the fact that she had allowed herself to be in a humiliating position. That entire night flashes of the journey of the last one decade with Pranav kept returning to her mind. His behavior in the last couple of these years, specifically so, after Sonal's entry, was beyond tolerance.

The next morning, Revathi walked up to Pranav, who still seemed to be recovering from the previous night's hangover.

"Pranav, even if you are partially in your senses, I want to have a talk with you."

"What is it about?"

"Pranav, I think, our problems are just getting insurmountable. I'd believe that before it's too late, we need to give each other a break. I think we must live separately or a while."

Pranav didn't know whether her caveat was for real. His head was still spinning. An hour later, when he settled down to feeling more normal, he realized that Revathi had already done her packing and was seriously planning to stay separately. Sure, it made for an unhappy family.

15

Painful Ecstasy – Part 2

It is indeed surprising how the prospect of parenthood pumps in a new lease of life into a married person's life. The feeling is almost akin to a second honeymoon. And Vishal and Gargi were now experiencing just that phase. There was a near paradigm shift in the way each behaved.

Vishal had now transformed into a dutiful, caring husband, who would call up his wife at least twice from the office just to check if all was well, whether she had had her meal and whether she was looking sexy enough to distract the neighbor's son. Gargi, too, would call him twice over. In the last couple of months, he never got swayed either; not that he did not come across attractive females but the thought of going ashtray seemed so alienating now. He was for a change the happily married guy for whom life revolved around just his work and home. Gargi had also learnt to accept her husband with some, if not all, of his failings and in fact quite liked them.

It was a Saturday morning and the couple was tempted by the prospect of a night out. An increment that Vishal had got in his salary recently added to the optimism. They decided to dine at the Olive at Bandra that night. After all, with parties at Olive being reported so often on Page 3 and even on NDTV's Mumbai Night Out, Gargi was quite keen to experience that milieu for herself; and Vishal, in his new avatar as the good, relenting husband couldn't possibly say no.

Vishal sauntered into the office a little later than usual and went straight to his workstation. He wanted to quickly wrap up the day's work so as to possibly take out an extra couple of hours and surprise his wife by returning home early. He was concentrating hard on an article when he got an SMS. The SMS was from Tina who was seated right across the table in front oh him. It read "Need to talk to you about something very urgent." Tina looked terribly hassled; her pout indicating that something was amiss.

Vishal went up to her.

"What's the matter, Tina?"

"I'm in deep shit, Vishal," she replied in a hushed tone.

"But what is the problem?"

"I can't discuss it here. It's very serious. I need to meet you alone."

Vishal realized that he had perhaps never seen Tina that shaken. Out of sheer humanly concern he decided to take her out for lunch. However, given the secretive nature of the problem, he realized he would have to scout for a restaurant where he wouldn't possibily bump into acquaintances. They ended up in a somewhat shady restaurant in the backside of Lokhandwala. Vishal placed the order quickly and got down to concentrating on what Tina had to speak.

"Now tell me, what is the matter?"

Tina looked guilty and was nearly speechless. She took a long pause before she finally spoke.

"Vishal, I'm pregnant."

Vishal couldn't believe his ears.

"What? What did you say?"

"Yes, I'm carrying."

Flashes of that wild afternoon in the hotel near Malad station stormed its way into Vishal's mind and hit him with a decimating impact.

"But I used a condom..." Vishal said defensively, thoroughly obfuscated by what he had heard.

"I know, Vishal. I'm not saying it's your child."

Vishal breathed a sigh of huge relief when Tina said this. Such was the feeling of relief that for a moment it did not bother him whose child it was. Perhaps at this point, even if he was told that Tina was a prostitute who had been sleeping around with multiple men, he wouldn't have been affected. Such indeed was his selfishness now on matters that did not concern him or his wife.

However, the Samaritan in him eventually got Tina to speak out.

"It is Girish's child," she revealed.

"What? But hadn't you broken off with him?"

"Yes, I had. But even after the break up he would plead with me to meet up again. Almost everyday he would call me and then beg me to put our differences behind and revive the relationship."

"What happened, then? Did you go back?"

"No, I didn't. I knew he was too whimsical for me to handle. At the same time, he wouldn't stop calling me. He created a situation where my father wanted to go to the police. But I stopped my father. I assured him that I will put an end to this drama."

"And what did you do?"

"I tried and reasoned out with Girish. I begged him, pleaded with him, cajoled and even shouted at him to get lost from my life. He agreed but on one condition. He wanted to make love to me one last time. He convinced me for it with all sorts of reasoning. He told me that we must celebrate our parting with one final act of sex and try and experience the same joy that we did the first time we had it. And he promised me several times over that the memories of this last experience would give him the courage to forget me and move out of my life forever."

"And you gave in?"

"Yes. And I did it not so much because I was buying peace from him. Somewhere, I realized that I too was thirsty to relive the ecstasy. He in fact took me to a hotel at Madh. But just before it all started, I realized that Girish did not have a condom. Though I insisted initially that he get one, he refused. He said that since it was the last time we were making love, he didn't want anything, not even a contraceptive to come between us. Girish was mad."

Vishal could sense that Tina was almost sucked in nostalgia as she narrated the tale. This, he gathered, was indicative of the fact that whatever she did, she'd have done with a lot of conviction. However, that conviction must have been lopsided; or else her fate would have been different.

"And you allowed yourself to be manipulated by his stupid logic and ended up being pregnant," Vishal concluded as though the conundrum was finally sorted out in his mind.

"Yes. I could have stopped him but I didn't. Somewhere I was a party to it. I too realized that perhaps it will be an experience I will cherish for all my life."

"Does Girish know that you are pregnant?"

"Yes, he does."

"What does he say?"

Tina's expression couldn't hide her anger at this stage.

"He refuses to accept that it is his child."

"What?"

"Girish asked me to prove that it's his child. He even accused me of sleeping around with men…"

Tina couldn't hold back her tears and ended up crying profusely.

'And do your parents know that you are pregnant?"

"No, they don't."

Vishal wondered how Tina could possibly have been so naïve. Or was she just cooking up a story? Was it possible by any means that the child was neither his nor Girish's? These thoughts couldn't possibly vanish in the smoke of Vishal's cigarette. They would haunt him for sure, he knew.

"Vishal I can't handle this any more. Hiding it from my parents has been damn tough… they'd actually got suspicious the first time I puked."

Vishal looked in complete disarray as Tina continued her sobbing.

"I just shudder to think of what my parents will go through when they get to know I'm pregnant. Oh, God, it's so tough on me that sometimes, I just feel like ending my life."

"But why don't you go for abortion? That looks like the only practical solution at this stage," Vishal spoke finally.

"I'm scared."

"Of what? Look, abortion is a very simple operation and you'll be normal within hours."

Tina thought for a moment.

"Vishal, will you please help me out with it? I can't trust anybody else with it. And I will need to have it done ASAP."

Vishal did not know what to say. He had never encouraged any proximity with Tina after their escapade. Hence, there was no perceptible reason why she should be showing such dependence on him now. But then, he was caught in a tricky situation. He couldn't possibly back out.

Was this by any means a ploy so that later Tina could blackmail him? Vishal wondered momentarily. She at least didn't look that vicious.

Vishal was clearly flummoxed. *How uncertain could life be*, he wondered. Just a couple of hours ago, Vishal couldn't possibly think beyond the proposed dinner with his wife. He had no idea that his lunch instead would be such a nightmare. Vishal bit his nails in sheer helplessness and then gave vent to his ire by blasting Girish. He couldn't do anything better in the state of mind he was in.

"I don't believe this. I mean I can't imagine that the guy for whom you fought with your own family did this to you. He must be such a swine… "

Strangely enough, Tina looked rather composed and normal when Girish was badmouthed. It was instead Vishal who appeared flabbergasted by Girish's perfidy.

"Give me the bastard's number. I'll talk to him right away."

Tina's silence finally gave in.

"No Vishal, I don't blame Girish for anything."

"What?" Vishal sounded more intrigued than ever. "Are you hiding something from me?"

There was a long pause. It seemed as though Tina was about to say something that was sure going to shake the world. And so it was.

"Vishal, I am a call girl."

Vishal wondered whether he was seeing a social thriller on TV. Tina's story surely had the elements of one.

Another half an hour had gone by. Vishal's shock was now replaced by resignation. He was beginning to come to terms with the fact that the charmer of his office was actually a call girl.

Vishal kept thinking about Tina's initiation into the trade much the way she had narrated it.

A college friend, Kamolika, had once unsuspectingly sent Tina off with a rich guy who she claimed was her friend. The rich guy took her home, made her see a porn DVD and then started to feel her. Before Tina could really protest, she was told that she'll be paid Rs. 5000 if she obeyed the guy for the next two hours. A 19 year old Tina, technically still a virgin – *she had only kissed and her boobs been fondled before* – gave in. She would have, even if she hadn't been offered money. But when the currency notes were actually put in her hand, she didn't mind it at all. Tina, at that point, had been contemplating taking up some part time job to augment her family's income. And this escapade didn't seem all that bad an option. Within a couple of weeks of her first experience, Tina came to believe that this was the best part time job she could think of. She did feel guilty every time she did it, but gradually the lure of money took precedence over the thirst for sex. Tina became more clinical in her approach; she ceased to even have a hangover. She learnt the ropes better alongside Kamolika and was soon able to trace wealthier clients who would even shell out Rs.10,000/- for a shot. With this, she was able to limit herself to feeling guilty only once in a month.

Vishal recalled having seen an expose on college girls taking to prostitution on Star News recently. He didn't know the girls looked as innocent as Tina.

Tina had been into this trade for a while before Girish walked into her life. Once they got into a relationship, she decided to end her paid escapades. Tina even stayed out of it for three months. But then a phase where her father went without employment for a while made her go back to the act. She would earn her bit and tell her parents that she was getting questionnaires filled for a market research firm.

Girish eventually got to know of her dark secret. He was not only hurt, but determined to teach her a lesson. And he did so by making her pregnant.

There were some discrepancies, though, in Tina's earlier version and her subsequent one. From what Vishal gathered, Girish couldn't have planned out her impregnation so meticulously. Though Girish and Tina were perhaps fighting for a while, they probably continued with their physical relationship all along, presumably so at Girish's behest. Or perhaps Girish wanted it that way till Tina became pregnant. What Vishal could not gather was what sort of a kick could Girish have got by doing so?

Vishal however left Tina's story at that. The more he thought about it, the more complicated it seemed, replete with unanswered puzzles. He chose instead to wash his hands off it.

Vishal, however, being the nice person he was, couldn't possibly leave Tina in the lurch, though he tried doing it. A couple of hours later, Vishal decided to take her to an abortion clinic. He called up a scribe friend of his who had recently reported on the spurt of such clinics and took out a couple of addresses. Vishal called up Gargi and informed her that he would be late since an important interview had come up. This was the first time he lied to her in months.

By 7:00pm, Tina's abortion got over at a shady Jaidev Maternity Clinic in the interiors of Sakinaka. Though Tina was yet to regain consciousness, Vishal decided to make a move, asking Kamolika, who was also there to take care of Tina from there on. He rushed home.

That night Vishal and Gargi dined at the Olive. Gargi experimented with at least three different varieties of exotic salads; Vishal opted for Biryani. Gargi had looked this happy only in their courtship days. And Vishal felt bad for that.

After dinner, the couple went on a long drive and reached the Hiranandani Gardens at Powai. The place seemed so fresh and exotic by Mumbai standards that Vishal drove round and round it for more than half an hour. Somewhere, at the back of his mind though, the unexpected incidents of the day involving Tina couldn't escape him. To be on the safer side, he had put his cell phone on the silent mode. The couple eventually landed home nearly at three in the morning.

The next day, Vishal woke up late, at around ten. He didn't find Gargi at home. He gathered she must have gone to buy fish, which they normally had for Sunday lunch. Vishal was still so tired that he slipped into slumber once again. When he finally woke up, it was well past noon, 2pm to be precise. Just as he opened his eyes, he saw an unusual sight. Gargi, properly dressed, was taking something out from the cupboard. She looked weak and low. Beside her, lay a huge suitcase, the one she used when she visited her parents at Meerut. Vishal, for a while didn't know if he was actually awake. He rubbed his eyes. He realized what he saw was no illusion.

"Hey Gargi, what's the matter?"

Gargi ignored him.

"What happened, Gargi? Are you going to meet your parents?"

"Yes…I'm going forever."

Vishal just couldn't gather anything. He looked all the more intrigued especially after the wonderful night they had had.

"For God's sake, Gargi, will you tell me, what is the matter?"

Gargi looked into his eyes with a conglomerated expression of hurt, betrayal, anger and venom. She just took Vishal's cell and gave it to him. Vishal had an inkling of what it could be. There was a message from Tina. It read: "Thanks a ton, Vishal, for the abortion. If the world had known about my pregnancy, I'd have killed myself."

The message was received early morning at 07:28:11. Due to the cell being on the silent mode, Vishal hadn't come to know of it.

Before Vishal could say a word, Gargi was prepared to rip him apart. And before Gargi's words could, her red eyes already spoke so much.

"I am really ashamed to call you my husband, Vishal. I always suspected you of being promiscuous and quite knew that you were. But the moment things seemed to improve, I put it all behind. I trusted you implicitly only to realize today what a double game you were up to."

"Gargi…"

"Oh, shut up. Don't you dare think of telling me another lie! I hate myself Vishal for having married a cheat like you. And today, I'm ending this marriage for good."

Gargi's temper was beyond control now, but she wasn't yet through.

"And yes, I have already ended whatever semblance of our relationship I was carrying. I went in the morning and got myself aborted."

Vishal trembled when she said this. He knew Gargi was crazy and capable of doing that.

16

The Inevitable

Revathi and Pranav were now separated. For most part of her ten-year long marriage, Revathi had shuddered at the vaguest fear of separation. She'd tell her friends that she'd rather die the day such a thing happened. Today, with her worst nightmare becoming a reality, life for her, seemed largely devoid of any direction or motive. She was alive though.

About the only silver lining for Revathi was the presence of Ria, who was staying with her.

Revathi had taken a small 1 BHK rental accommodation in Juhu. With minimal furniture and hardly any enthusiasm to do up her house, she lived each day as it came.

Mayank's involvement in Revathi's life quite naturally grew. He would drop in at her place almost every evening now and call her up about half a dozen times during the day. While the conversations resulted invariably from his concern for her, Ria was gradually beginning to hate him. The kid would feel an intense animosity each time she would see Mayank in the house. Ria would suddenly become crotchety and start shouting and throwing things around. "Can't you both keep shut? I'm getting disturbed," Ria would scream abruptly.

Revathi knew enough of child psychology to understand why

Ria behaved thus. She felt guilty and hence for Ria's sake tried reducing Mayank's involvement in her life. She would at times not take his call especially when Ria was around. At other times, Revathi would avoid meeting by cooking up an alibi.

Revathi wondered how ironical life could be. Ria, after all, now had to go through the same emotional trauma that Revathi, in her childhood had and something that Revathi had resolved never to let her daughter experience. At times, Revathi even contemplated ending all contact with Mayank. On second thoughts, she was not too sure if Mayank deserved to be squarely blamed for all her problems.

Pranav, on the other hand, too, shifted out of their Lokhandwala home. He possibly couldn't bear to live in the house alone; Revathi's absence haunted him. He was in a turbulent mental state. While he felt a strong indignation towards Revathi for letting Mayank enter her life, the indignation was more the sort parents feel when they see their kids in bad company. Pranav also wondered if in these last ten years, he had, at all, managed to shed being in the parental mould in so far as his relationship with Revathi went. This was a strong fear one of Pranav's closest buddies had sounded him out on, during Pranav's courtship days. After all, the age gap between Pranav and Revathi was significant.

In Revathi's absence however, Pranav felt a strange reassurance about her. He was quite optimistic that six months down the line all would be well. It was ironical that he hadn't felt this reassured and optimistic while she was still with him. But then, that was the kind of trust he had in her, which, at one point had made him take a fancy for her without knowing her at all. The male chauvinist in him did shudder at the prospect of Revathi and Mayank consummating their relationship in this period. But Ria's presence with Revathi allayed such fears partially.

As time flew, Mayank's marriage date was now just about three weeks away. His parents, in fact, had landed up in Mumbai to shop with him for the occasion. His parents came to know of Revathi, who they were told was a "professional friend". They were least bothered.

Since Mayank would be really occupied during the day, he made up by talking to Revathi over a long telephonic conversation at night. This conversation was more or less a routine affair and would even go on for well more than an hour. Mayank would virtually lock himself in his room when this conversation happened. His parents did not mind it much as they thought it was Rewa who he talked with.

One day, however Rewa called up early to wish Mayank's mother a Happy Birthday. Rewa sounded worried that day.

"Aunty I hope all is well with Mayank. I kept trying his cell till late into the night but it was switched off. I tried the residence number but it was continuously engaged."

"What? He was talking to someone on the phone last night. I thought that was you..."

Mayank's Mom was intrigued. She'd been thinking all this while that it was Rewa who he religiously talked with at nights. If it wasn't Rewa, then who was it?

"Revathi," Mayank admitted.

"What?"

"Yes, she is a friend...a very dear friend of mine," Mayank confessed. There was an underlying tinge of possessiveness and an undercurrent of rebellion in his speech when he spoke of Revathi. And that only rattled his parents.

"Yeah... but if I remember correctly, you never really had close female friends and now just before your marriage..."

Mayank's Mom cut his Dad short.

"Besides, she is much older. Why do you need this intimate friendship at this stage?"

Mayank felt embarrassed enough to just go off abruptly.

Mayank confided in Revathi about his parents discovering their relationship. Strangely it was sympathy that it evoked from Revathi and not empathy, as he had hoped.

"You have really brought this upon yourself Mayank. Even now you have time. Just forget me. It will do you a world of good."

Mayank was shocked to hear this; he didn't know why. Perhaps he was still subconsciously hoping in his heart of hearts that Revathi would come around to the idea of accepting him. But that, with these words of hers, seemed impossible now.

Now barely a little over two weeks was left for his marriage. The inherent restlessness that Mayank always experienced when he thought of Revathi hadn't ceased though. He tried reconciling to Revathi's counsel, but it wasn't easy. And he wondered why. Sure, there must been an "unachieved agenda", as Anil would have him believe. Perhaps, he would have at least wanted to consummate their relationship. After all, Mayank knew he might never experience the fulfillment in Rewa that he always found in Revathi.

But then not all wishes are destined to be fulfilled; Mayank thought. He again took solace in Sahir Ludhianvi's elegiac summary of the situation:

Taruf (feelings) rog ho jaye to usko bhulna behtar,
Taluk (relationship) bojh ban jaye to usko todana achacha
Woh afasana jise anjam tak lana na ho mumkin,
Use ek khubsoorat mod dekar chhodana achcha..

Perhaps Sahir must have gone through something similar, Mayank surmised.

Mayank's parents soon left for Indore. He was supposed to join them a couple of days before the marriage date. That evening when Mayank saw off his parents at the railway station, he felt unusually forlorn. Perhaps, because the only other person in the city he had come close enough to calling family had been avoiding him too.

Something propelled Mayank to drive straight to Revathi's place. It was almost seven by the time he reached her place. Mayank arrived outside her door, but something prevented him from directly ringing the bell; he wasn't sure how he would be received. Thrice he raised his finger to ring the bell and thrice he withdrew it. On one occasion he even turned back and thought of leaving but then turned again and rang the bell. It took Revathi quite a while to open the door. The place was nearly all dark, her hair unkempt and strewn all across; she had apparently been sitting alone near the window. Mayank was in a bit of shock.

"Are you alright?"

"Yeah…I am." Her voice sounded choked.

Revathi did not seem surprised to see Mayank. She instead looked relieved. She just walked in expecting Mayank to follow, as if she had anticipated he would come. Mayank was a little surprised as he had instead anticipated an adverse reaction.

"What's the matter, Revathi? Why is it all dark?"

"There isn't anything bright happening in life, anyway. I just wanted it this way."

Mayank was about to switch the light on, when Revathi stopped.

"Let it be like this for sometime. There is some light coming in from outside."

Mayank knew that Revathi must have been terribly depressed. There weren't many reasons why she wouldn't be.

"Where is Ria? "

"Ria has gone to a friend's place. She'll be staying there tonight."

Revathi had never sounded so low. For a few moments, neither of them spoke a word. Revathi had gone back to sitting on a chair placed next to the window and stared outside with a near blank expression. Mayank just witnessed it helplessly before he went to her and held her shoulders supportively. Revathi looked up into his eyes; there were tears in hers. Within moments, she broke down completely and Mayank consoled her like he would a kid.

"Mayank, what have I done to deserve all this? Why is God being so unfair upon me?"

Mayank too was nearly in tears by now, feeling guilty.

"Look Revathi, we have done nothing… I just care…"

Revathi cut him short.

"I know we have not done anything. You are quite inconsequential Mayank in all that has happened between Pranav and me. People are merely catalysts… they can lead to a situation; they can't be the situation. But it's the situation more than the individual that's responsible. I guess if all had been well between Pranav and me, I wouldn't have even interacted so much with you."

Mayank carefully heard her out. At the end, he did feel somewhat exonerated. But that again did not sort the "situation" out and as he too believed now, it was the situation more than individual that was killing him from within.

"Revathi, I think you were right. Perhaps I had been impulsive not to listen to you. But till the time we keep meeting, I'm sure the situation can never improve for any of us."

Revathi looked at him a bit surprised even as Mayank continued.

"You know what when I came here today, I didn't exactly know what brought me here. Perhaps all along I've been escaping from the realities of my life and seeking shelter in you. And before you start doing the same, I think we really need to move on."

Revathi looked surprised. She found it tough to believe that the confused kid she knew had grown overnight. Or maybe, not overnight, the last few months that they'd known each other must have been his journey into coming of age.

"I'm so glad for you, Mayank. I don't know whether I should be saying this but at times, you remind me so much of Pranav. I mean the spells of extreme immaturity followed by those of extreme maturity."

Revathi sounded choked as she spoke and it gave Mayank a sense of the gamut of emotions she'd been experiencing.

That evening, they decided to visit the Siddivinayank Temple and seek divine blessings before bidding each other a final adieu. However, half way through the journey, Revathi was tormented by the memories of that evening nearly 11 years ago when Pranav and she had made a similar journey.

"Mayank, can we go somewhere else?"

Mayank, as always, was intelligent enough to know why Revathi said this.

"Hmmm... Well... Haji Ali?"

They reached the Haji Ali at almost 9. By then, the rush had decreased and a nice breeze was blowing softly. As Mayank and Revathi traveled the narrow stretch of land leading them on to the *dargah*, they experienced a rare solitude from the world. It was a moment that Mayank wished could stay with them forever.

After paying obeisance at the dargah, they went behind the

shrine. It was a desolate sort of balcony, less frequented by visitors. When Mayank and Revathi stood there, they almost felt a sense of loss. After all, these were perhaps the last few moments they were spending together. Without uttering a word, they reflected upon their unusual bond. Mayank then, held her hand and led her to the rocks that edged the sea. He sat there, Revathi beside him. The waves that hit these rocks, invariably splashed unto their clothes but they did not mind. They spent nearly twenty minutes there, neither saying a word, each feeling a rare empathy for the other. This silence was perhaps the most telling interaction they ever had.

At a little beyond half past 9, they finally decided to leave. The stretch of land leading to the dargah was now even more deserted, except for the presence of some beggars who resorted to unusual antics to draw their attention. Perhaps they too were tired and hence frivolous.

Suddenly from the other side, a couple, along with a small kid, could be seen rushing in. In less than a moment, in order to avoid an intrusive beggar, the couple actually swayed over to the other side and the woman bumped straight into Mayank. She held her four year old or so son's hand.

"I'm sorry. I'm really sorry," said the woman, controlling the kid and looking up.

Mayank was stunned to see her. It was a familiar face, the glow diminished though. Perhaps some amount of fat had accumulated on it. The dressing was more sedate, the demeanor more restrained. The hair was not as long as they used to be. They went till just about beneath the shoulder. The voice sounded huskier or maybe more encumbered. But the eyes had the same depth. The person was the same – Shweta.

For a few seconds, Mayank and Shweta just looked at each other in abject disbelief. They sure wanted to speak but the gamut of memories that resurfaced out of the blue had numbed them completely. They were both struggling for words. And then Shweta realizing her husband's awkwardness broke the ice.

"Sharad, this is Mayank and Mayank this is my husband, Sharad."

They shook hands.

"Meet Revathi my friend. Revathi, this is Shweta."

Revathi looked stunned at the bizarre coincidence. She knew what Shweta had meant for Mayank.

"Looks like you both know each other well," Sharad quipped.

Both Shweta and Mayank looked at each other awkwardly. "No, we were just together in college," Mayank said rather impersonally.

"It's such a pleasant surprise Mayank." Shweta was more exuberant.

"Yeah, good to see you after ages and I must say you've got a very cute little kid," Mayank retorted formally.

"Actually we're on a short vacation to India and since Sharad has some relatives here, we thought we'd stay here for a couple of days. Mayank, aren't you married?"

Mayank was taken aback by the suddenness of this unwanted query. However, he quickly gathered himself.

"Of course, I am." Mayank's confusion had made it all the more apparent to Shweta that he wasn't. She instead chose to change the topic.

"Hey, it's been ages… Let's catch up sometime tomorrow… What say, Sharad?"

Before Sharad could say anything, Mayank did.

"Actually tomorrow, I'm off to Delhi for some work."

Mayank was rather dispassionate and Shweta noticed it. She knew the cause and all she could possibly feel was guilt.

That evening as they drove back, Mayank was unusually silent. It wasn't difficult for Revathi to know what was going on in his mind.

"Hey, are you okay?"

Mayank had a wry smile.

"It's so strange Revathi that people are always trapped in wrong selections."

"What do you mean?"

"I could easily make out that Shweta can never feel for her husband the way she still feels for me."

Revathi wasn't too surprised to hear this. She had long got used to Mayank's impertinent and sweeping statements. Only, she didn't know where they emanated from.

That night they had sandwiches at Revathi's place that were ordered from Subway. And then Mayank finally got up to leave.

"Take care, Revathi. I'll miss you a lot."

"You too. And be happy."

They hugged each other; the spontaneity in the act was such that it wasn't clear who initiated the gesture. It was their first hug and what a bear hug it was.

Mayank finally turned to leave. Revathi followed him to the door. Revathi, this time around was more tentative in her movements than him. Just as he reached the door, she placed her hand on his shoulder, still seeming uncertain and nervous. Mayank turned. There was a glint of the unexpected in Revathi's eyes, something Mayank couldn't recall having seen before. There was suspense. She looked straight into his eyes and then brought herself closer to Mayank. Mayank didn't know what was happening, nor was he too keen to know. He was simply enjoying the moment. Revathi made her lips gently touch his and gave him a soft peck.

For a moment, Mayank didn't know if what he'd seen of Revathi in the last five minutes or so was his fantasy or if it was for real. But yes he did feel something on his lips; they were wet and simply yearning for another such feel. On an impulse, Mayank just reciprocated the act. He did it far more passionately and the two lip-locked hard.

The act had brought about a sudden spurt in Mayank's hormones. He started unbuttoning Revathi's top. Revathi pulled herself away and turned the other way. Mayank was taken aback. He felt guilty. For a while, both were quiet. Mayank had begun to retreat, when Revathi went back to him. She looked into his eyes. Mayank could read hers. He knew that Revathi had perhaps consented.

Within moments, they were locked in passionate love making. Interestingly, for most part, Revathi was the more enterprising partner, guiding Mayank with a whole lot of nuances that she'd learnt from Pranav over the years. She quite liked fondling his penis and even guided it to fuck her boobs. When Mayank did so, positioning himself right on top of her, he was reminded of a conversation they very recently had had. He got off and placed himself right beside her. He looked into her eyes mischievously, even as he caressed her hair. "Do I still remind you of Pranav?"

It was a weird sort of question, at a time when Revathi seemed just about able to not think of Pranav. She gave him another peck, but looked somewhat indifferent this time around. Mayank got the message; sure she didn't want to be reminded of Pranav at this hour. He soon got on with the act and then concentrated on the lower parts of her body – the thighs and the butt to be more precise. He kissed and bit them with great finesse.

And in a finale, when Mayank did penetrate her, he just clung on to her for a long time. The act was so intense that both were completely bathed in sweat; yet they seemed to thoroughly enjoy each other's odor.

Mayank kissed her on her forehead, she kissed him on his eyebrows, he kissed her eyelashes, she kissed him below the eyes, he kissed her nose, she kissed his lips, he kissed hers, she kissed his chin, he kissed her neck. He started to take off her clothes with utmost care. Revathi did not protest one bit. He then kissed her armpit, she kissed his nipple, he kissed her navel ... For a long while thereafter, they just lay by each other's side, caressing and feeling each other. They showered affection in abundance, rapt completely in the surprise of all that was happening.

And then they got locked in passionate love making ... They made love till the wee hours of the morning.

"Thanks, Revathi. I need to thank you for this."

Revathi awaited a clearer explanation.

"Thanks for making me lose my virginity."

Revathi didn't know what he was saying but he went on.

"Shweta had never let me go beyond a kiss. She was too much of a behenji on these matters. And I'd waited all these years to gift my virginity to someone I really love. And here I am… I'm glad you made me fulfill my wish."

Revathi was just too shocked. The guy never quite ceased to surprise her.

17

Coming of Age

It was early morning. Dawn was just about breaking when Revathi, virtually unable to sleep all night, got up from her bed. She moved to her window. The scene of the dawn breaking was something she had not seen in years. Perhaps the last time she saw it was nearly four years ago, when Pranav and she were holidaying in Mahabaleshwar. A late night conversation then had snowballed into a major argument that kept them awake the whole night. Revathi wanted another baby, Pranav was dead against it.

Today it wasn't quite a skirmish; it was a crisis of another kind. She had made love to a man other than Pranav – something she'd never thought would happen. And it wasn't quite forced upon her; rather it was something she perhaps subconsciously wanted. Now it was about four hours from the time that the act had got over. Strangely enough, Revathi didn't hate herself. She was experiencing a feeling she didn't recall having experienced before— liberation. That was the effect that corporal indulgence had in her; she was feeling emotionally and sexually liberated. Her innermost dispositions reeked more of reconciliation than revulsion; and this surprised her no end.

Revathi stood motionless at her window, when to her surprise she saw Pranav arrive in his car. She wondered why he had to come at this weird hour.

Revathi quickly washed her face. Pranav rang the doorbell. Revathi pretended to look surprised as she opened the door.

"Pranav?"

"Yeah. Just felt like meeting Ria."

Pranav looked completely unsure of himself. It was like he uttered something whereas there was something entirely different going on in his mind.

"Ria is at a friends' place... but do come in."

Pranav followed Revathi as she walked in. A few minutes later, they sat over morning tea. Each was intrigued to see the other completely lost and fumbling for words. Something was amiss, neither knew what it was.

"So how is Sonal?"

Pranav, at first, was shocked to hear this. Was it natural for Revathi to think that if they were not together, Pranav would be with Sonal? He wondered. Well yes, the frequency of their meetings had increased and they'd even spent the last weekend in Goa, but Pranav was still far from seeing any marital worth in Sonal. On the other hand, spending more time with Sonal had only made him realize the worth of Revathi all the more.

Pranav's inability to answer made Revathi let go of the question.

"How's that guy, Mayank?" Pranav asked rather diffidently. His tenor was probing though.

"Okay," she replied rather curtly. "Listen Pranav, will you just wait for a while? I'll take a shower and come. I'm feeling uncomfortable."

Revathi went off, carrying a towel. Pranav felt strange. A dignified distance or rather the obligation to be respectfully formal had crept into their relationship. Pranav felt a little restless while Revathi was away. He walked to and fro. Without really being conscious of it, he stepped into Revathi's bedroom. He was shocked to see it in the state it was in. The bed sheet looked violently disturbed. He was sure Revathi wouldn't have hopped on it all night. Sure there must have been some 'intense activity'. And then on one side of the bed table was what left no doubt in his mind about it must have been – a male handkerchief. He knew his wife was no longer a 'virgin' outside marriage.

Pranav walked out of the room, his steps heavy and defeated. And just as he reached the door, there was Revathi in front of him, just out of her bath. Pranav held the handkerchief in his hand, without quite realizing he did so. The deafening silence that prevailed between them said more than words ever could. It was as if both were speaking to each other by their expressions and eye contact (or rather the lack of it). Verbal communication followed.

"So you did it last night?"

Revathi almost did not respond and then nodded. A long pause followed. Revathi was surprised by how calm Pranav seemed. Or was it just a façade?

"How was it?"

Revathi looked confused for a moment. How was what...the carnal act? She did not answer, even as Pranav kept looking into her eyes, hoping to elicit an answer.

"Did he satisfy you? You enjoyed it?"

"Enough, Pranav," she shouted, indignation writ large on her.

Pranav laughed almost derisively. It couldn't instantly be made out whether the derision was aimed at Revathi's act or his own condition. And then, he suddenly hugged her hard. Revathi just stood confused, clasped in the hug. She knew for sure that Pranav was not normal; his behavior now was alarming enough to need urgent psychiatric help.

⤸

Mayank too felt different. The act had a cathartic effect on him; he felt unburdened to a great extent. After all, he had experienced the fear of having to live with the "unachieved agenda". For him it was a triumph of sorts, a triumph that eventually did not need him to slog much. He was aware, though, that in his victory perhaps lay Revathi's biggest defeat; or was it so? He wasn't too sure today. Revathi too might have been feeling triumphant in ways, he thought.

Mayank's date of marriage was now just 10 days away. He had even got the possession of his new Mindspace flat. His mind however was blanker than ever. He just didn't seem to know what to do next. That evening Mayank called up his parents.

"Mom, I don't want to go ahead with this marriage."

"What? Do you know what you're saying?"

"Yeah…I'm just not feeling up to it."

"You've gone mad," Mom flared.

"I have. But listen, Mom, what I said is final. I'm not marrying Rewa." Mayank just disconnected abruptly. He was breathing almost violently and looked disturbed like someone lost completely in chaos.

His parents had had an inkling that this could happen. They were numbed by its impact, though.

Mayank sent an SMS to Revathi. It read: "I've called off my marriage." He'd perhaps deliberately left it abrupt, like usual, hoping that Revathi would call. She didn't. He didn't bother much either, choosing to give her more time to possibly recover from what had happened between them.

The next evening Mayank shifted to his new Mindspace flat. It was his most lonely evening in years. Vishal and Anil did join him late in the evening but this gathering looked more like a condolence meet. The whisky, instead of pepping up their spirits, immersed them deeper into melancholy.

"You think Revathi will marry you?" Anil asked gently. Mayank said nothing. He was lost somewhere, perhaps thinking of the dramatic chain of incidents that had unfolded between him and Revathi in the past few months.

Vishal looked livid. "You know what Mayank, this lady... what's her name... Revathi... she has just destroyed you. She has left you good for nothing. You're neither here nor there," Vishal blabbered.

Anil just tapped Vishal's shoulder indicating that he must shut up.

Vishal however went on, "Hey, dude, come on; be practical. Women like her are what you call coquettes; of course a guy like me would call them cock teasers."

That insinuation was sufficient to annoy Mayank to the extent that he just pulled Vishal by his collar. The evening ended on a sour note.

The next morning Vishal, out of his concern for Mayank chose to forget the unpleasantness of the previous night. He instead persuaded Mayank to come along with him to a Tarot reader. Vishal had started believing in Tarot reading lately.

As they sat with the Tarot reader, an elegant lady in her early fifties, the lady after an initial look at the set of three cards that she had picked, cautioned Mayank, "There's somebody close to you who is harming you a lot."

Mayank was shocked to hear this. "But who?"

"Well, we can try to find that out."

"How?"

"You can mention the names of people you have suspicion on and I can ask the powers if the said person is the 'one'."

"But I don't have suspicion on anyone."

At this point Vishal intervened, "Look, what you do is start naming all your friends- Anil, Vishal, Revathi one by one. Let's find out who it is."

Mayank found the whole exercise quite weird. Moreover it put him in an extremely awkward position. What if the 'powers' were to actually confirm that one of his close friends was harming him?

"Come on, son. Knowing the evil will only help you,' quipped the lady.

Left with no option, Mayank started dropping names. Understandably so, Mayank mentioned the name of Vishal first. For every name mentioned, the lady would ask the question to the 'powers' and pick out three cards. Depending on which these three cards were she would interpret the answer.

All went off well till Vishal made Mayank mention Revathi's name. The lady picked out three cards. She looked worried in an unusual sort of way. From the peep that Mayank could manage into the cards, he saw some demonic incarnation in one of them.

"God! It's this lady."

"What?"

"The powers tell me she is so vicious. She has a double face. She can't mean any good to you."

Mayank was shocked. His instant reaction was to give Vishal a glare as if to say what was this nonsenseVishal had led him to. Mayank simply walked off abruptly without uttering a word.

That night Mayank was restless. He kept thinking about what the Tarot card reader had said. Why had Revathi still not responded to his message whereby he informed her about his decision to call off marriage? Will Revathi marry him? These questions rattled him, as he knew the answer lay in the bosom secrets of Revathi that he still wasn't quite privy to. A woman's mind could never ever be read, he concluded.

It was midnight, but Mayank simply couldn't contain himself. He picked up his cell and called Revathi. He didn't know what he would say but some answers he definitely wanted. Revathi was woken up from her sleep by his call.

"Revathi, what do you feel about me?"

"What do you mean?"

"What if I were to tell you now that I want to marry you tomorrow?"

Revathi took a long pause.

"Mayank, I think we spoke about it once. And you know what my answer will be."

"Oh, come on, Revathi, that was a different situation. Now, it's different. You're not with Pranav, besides we... we consummated."

That was sufficient to irritate Revathi.

"Look Mayank, let's not get into that."

"Why?"

"What do you mean why? Stay within your limits."

"Look Revathi, I want to marry you. And I mean it."

Revathi was stunned by these words yet again.

"Then get this clear, that will never ever happen. Not till I'm alive."

The words sprang in Mayank's ears in the most jarring way.

"Fine, let me just fuck you again." Mayank blurted out in mad exasperation.

"What?' Revathi couldn't believe her ears.

"Yes, I said I wanna fuck you again. Trust me this time you'll enjoy it even more."

"To hell with you! This is the last time that we speak. Never ever call me again…"

Revathi banged the phone. Mayank must have called her at least a dozen times, but she did not pick it up. That night Mayank cried. Was the Tarot reader right? Had he been in love with a "vicious woman with a double face"? Mayank cried like a kid the whole night, just like he had when he was told several years ago that Shweta had been married off to someone else.

When dawn broke, strangely enough, Mayank felt fresh rather than drained out. The freshness stemmed out of the hope that his incessant weeping may have perhaps exorcized another aborted relationship from his system. Yes, he wanted to move on. He was feeling prepared to start life afresh. He was confident he could do so.

⌒

Two Years Later…

The first rains had lashed the city a few hours ago. Another Monsoon was just about setting in. The gentle drizzle outside made the weather hopelessly romantic.

Revathi however lay on her sofa in a rather somber mood. Pranav and she had finally obtained divorce about a week back. This was after spending a good one year in their second spell, trying hard to make their marriage work. However, within weeks of getting back together, they had begun to believe that their relationship was all but over. Temperament and personality clashes had led to a very disturbed scenario at home. Each looked like a complete stranger to the other. For the sake of Ria, they clung on for a while till they eventually got her admitted in a boarding school. Once that happened, the couple decided to part ways conclusively.

Today with the onset of another monsoon, a strange, long forgotten thought somehow lurked in Revathi's mind. The thought was of a bygone Monsoon and of an interesting entity the rains had brought along. She was somehow reminded of Mayank, whom she hadn't spoken to in ages. Not after that animated midnight conversation on the phone. She was somehow just missing him, she didn't know why. Not that she wanted to revive anything, but she just seemed inquisitive to know where and how Mayank was. She felt unusually nostalgic, she didn't know why.

Revathi called up Mayank on his cell. The number did not exist. Revathi was worried. She called up his office. The receptionist informed her that Mayank had quit his job. The receptionist had no clue where he was currently working. Strangely enough Revathi felt scared; a strange fear loomed in her mind, a fear of something being seriously amiss. In her anxiety, Revathi called up the office again and took Mayank's address, reasoning out that she was his cousin. It was only after she had completed the call that she realized how childish she had been. Nonetheless, she did not mind. She still felt scared; something in her propelled her to just take the car keys -*yeah the last two years' hardships had even made her learn how to drive*- and head towards Mayank's address.

Revathi arrived outside Mayank's building. She remembered it was the same building that Mayank was supposed to buy a flat in long ago. The flat though was not the one that she had rejected.

233

He'd brought her there for her opinion, in the days when she'd be his 'agony aunt'.

Revathi reached the eighth floor where his flat was. She rang the bell. As she waited for the door to be opened, she felt damn nervous. The door was opened by a male servant.

"Yes…"

"Uhh…"

"You've come to meet Saheb?"

Revathi simply nodded.

"Come, Saheb will be back any moment. He's asked me to take care of any of his friends who come in his absence."

Revathi walked, a little surprised by the warmth shown by the servant to a complete stranger.

Revathi sat for a while. The rains were now heavier. Perhaps they were setting the right feel for something so passionate, as this meeting between two unusual lovers. Or so she felt. By now Revathi's heartbeat had increased considerably. She was shaky like a teenager who'd fallen in love for the first time. She realized the wait for seeing Mayank was only making her anxiety grow. How would he look like? Would he have put on weight – a thing he dreaded? What will he do when he sees her first… hug her, smile, embrace…? Oh, she just didn't have a clue.

The feel of Mayank putting his head on her lap in a rather 'testing' sort of way the last time she'd come into his flat, seemed so fresh in her mind. It was as if the incident had occurred just a while back. Would he choose to do it again today? Well, if he did, she knew she wouldn't mind him ogling at her from that position today. Almost every minute Revathi looked at her watch, unable to decipher the cause for her madness.

And then the wait got over. Mayank stood right in front of her eyes. No, he hadn't put on weight. He looked younger and better than ever. In fact, he wore a formal suit – a marked improvement from the casual dressing he was accustomed to. No, he didn't embrace her or hug her. He didn't look particularly happy on seeing her either. He had a rather faint, forced sort of smile on his face. He didn't seem to be sure whether he ought to smile or not.

Revathi on the other hand was excited. It seemed as though Mayank and she had swapped positions in these two years.

"Hey, Mayank, how are you?" she beamed in joy and moved towards him, unmindful completely of her body language.

However, she had to stop herself mid-way. Another woman seemed to stake claim over Mayank.

"Oh Gosh, Mayank… What sort of neighbor you have? She wasn't letting me come." A woman entered from behind Mayank, oblivious of the presence of Revathi. The woman, clad in a maroon saree, was a lot younger and as pretty if not prettier than Revathi. An awkward silence descended upon the room, till Mayank broke it.

"Sonia, this is Revathi. And Revathi this is my wife. We just got married in the court today."

Revathi was zapped. She had an inkling that something was 'seriously amiss'. Or perhaps it was bad timing. Oh, so this is what it was. She found it hard to exude her natural smile. She again didn't exactly know why. After all, she'd always wished and wanted that Mayank get married. Perhaps in this long hiatus, certain dormant feelings had subconsciously been ignited. She didn't know why and when it happened. And what wrong timing it was!

Sonia looked damn gorgeous. She seemed intelligent too and of course was many years younger. Mayank had always been on the lookout for that elusive combination of 'intellect and beauty' and here he seemed to have finally got it. Was this by any means causing Revathi envy? Revathi did not know.

"Congratulations to both of you," Revathi uttered shakily, seeming only a shadow of her graceful self.

"Thanks."

"I think I've come at a wrong time. I'll catch up with you later."

"Don't be so formal, Ma'am. At least have some sweets before you go," Sonia insisted.

It was apparent from the way Sonia spoke that she'd been told about Revathi.

"No, no. I'll see you again. "

"Come on ma'am. Just be seated. Why don't you and Mayank talk? I'll get something for you." Sonia went in leaving Mayank and Revathi alone.

Mayank was unusually silent. Perhaps the hurt still remained.

"Mayank, I'm very happy for you. But somehow I'm feeling very awkward at this point. Listen I'll leave before Sonia comes. Just tell her I was not feeling well, okay," Revathi tried taking him into confidence like she'd do in the past.

Mayank did not say anything; he just looked on.

"Bye." Revathi left.

When Sonia came out with sweets, she wasn't surprised so much by Revathi leaving as she was by her arriving there in the first place.

"Why had she come here?" she asked Mayank. Mayank was trying to find the answer himself.

When Revathi reached her car, she realized that in her haste, she'd left her cell phone behind. She didn't have an option but to go back and collect it though she would have loved to avoid going back.

Revathi went up to Mayank's flat. The door wasn't completely closed. She was just about to ring the bell when she overheard Mayank and Sonia talk.

"I have absolutely no idea why Revathi came here. That's as much a puzzle for me as it is for you. In fact, I'd never hoped to see her again."

"It's okay, darling. I hope it hasn't upset you so much."

Mayank took a long pause before he went on.

"You know Sonia, certain relationships are doomed. They are meant to give you agony and pain, nothing else. Usually these relationships can't be defined; hence they don't have a name. They're just destined. I mean that's how accidents happen and you meet the wrong people, right?"

Sonia just tapped his shoulder, sensing her husband's anguish. The words seemed to have deafened Revathi, with their ugly impact.

"Sonia, today I want to erase that chapter from my life forever. Yes, I wish I had never met Revathi."

Revathi couldn't take it any more. She just walked off, the words resonating violently in her ears.

"Tumhe bhi yaad nahi aur main bhi bhool gaya,
Woh lamha kitna haseen tha, magar fuzool gaya"
- Javed Akhtar in Tarkash

Three hours had gone by. Even as it drizzled continuously, Revathi was lost in a peculiar activity. She'd been driving her car relentlessly, up and down the Western Express Highway, ever since she came out of Mayank's building. She'd completed four rounds and seemed to have the energy for more. Perhaps she had nothing better to do. Revathi didn't want to return to the forlorn confines of her home – not so early. The words of Mayank seemed like the unkindest cut of all. But Revathi was still happy. She felt reassured. The confused kid she'd met in these rains, exactly three monsoons ago had finally grown into a mature adult. So what if the transformation had made him wish 'that he'd never met Revathi.'

That night, even as it kept raining, Mayank stood on his terrace. Sonia was asleep. Mayank felt strange. The images of a shaken and nervous Revathi just wouldn't leave him. He was apparently fulfilled, yet empty. Tears rolled down his face and converged into the rain drops. He cried. Only he knew that contrary to what he made everybody believe, he could never grow out of Revathi.